The Bachelor in

ATLANTIS

LEIGH WYNDFIELD

OMNIFIC PUBLISHING

LOS ANGELES

Omnific Publishing
2355 Westwood Blvd., Suite 506
Los Angeles, CA 90064

www.omnificpublishing.com

First Omnific eBook edition, June 2022
First Omnific trade paperback edition, June 2022

The characters and events in this book are fictitious.
Any similarity to real persons, living or dead,
is coincidental and not intended by the author.

Library of Congress Cataloguing-in-Publication Data

Wyndfield, Leigh.

The Bachelor in Space / Leigh
Wyndfield – 1st ed. ISBN: 978-1-
623422-74-5

1. Contemporary Romance —
Fiction. 2. Adventure — Fiction.

3. Science Fiction — Fiction. 4. Humor — Fiction. I. Title

10 9 8 7 6 5 4 3 2 1

Cover and Interior Design by Sweet n' Spicy Designs
Printed in the United States of America

CHAPTER ONE

*J*ackson Wright no longer looked like a god.

In his headshots as this season's newest Bachelor, Jackson's long, golden hair and classic chiseled features were surrounded by a halo of light in every promotional photograph. He'd been the spitting image of a modern-day Thor. Sugar was sure women across the world had taken one look at him and swooned.

Yet here he stood on the first day of filming with his locks shorn off and his hair appearing more light brown than glowing blond. Sugar wasn't personally a fan of long-haired men, since in her opinion they tended not to take care of it properly, which led to split ends and greasy roots. But while he might be more attractive to her own personal tastes, she was sure Bachelor fans were going to be sorely disappointed.

Sadly, the damage had been done. Hair couldn't be glued back together again. Although a wig… No, men in wigs were too obvious.

Sugar had no doubt that when Hank Carson, the show's producer, saw Jackson's hair, a thunderstorm would rain down upon him. Luckily, she was not in charge of the Bachelor's hair. At least, she didn't think she was. This was her first time as Head Wrangler on the show and she wasn't completely sure of her responsibilities, since her contract stated that ultimately she was responsible for "timely filming completion," which meant she was really responsible for everything.

Before she could ask about his poor hairstyle choices, the elevator they would take into Atlantis dinged, signaling its arrival. The doors whisked open and she, Russ the camera-man, and the Bachelor trooped aboard. They were the first group of many that were on their way down into the watery depths a hundred feet below the surface of Lake Superior to one of the hottest attractions on Earth.

Russ pushed the button marked "Atlantis" and the doors closed, beginning the most important job of her career.

Standing next to each other, Russ and the new bach-elor couldn't be more opposite. Russ looked like a gamer with his pale skin and shaggy clothes. Jackson, looming over both of them in a manly male kind of way, gave off the superhero vibe that didn't seem to be an act on his part, even dressed as he was more for a boardroom than a theme park.

Jackson certainly filled out his suit in all the right ways, although there was something about the hipster cut of the pants and jacket that were slightly awkward on him, as if someone else had dressed him. Since costuming chose all the clothes for the talent, she figured they had picked this ensem-ble out as well.

She had to admit that even if he didn't look like Thor, he was still above-average handsome. Just now it was more of a businessman kind of way or an engineer, which she guessed made sense since he'd been an engineer on the space station last season, which was where Hank had found him. Hank had taken one look at Jackson Wright and had known he was Bachelor material. Although that had been before the haircut.

The doors closed and the elevator jerked violently as it started down, throwing her across the small space. Her extra high heeled boots, while beautiful, gave her no purchase as she scrambled for footing. To her left, Russ barely saved him-self from a bad fall by grabbing the railing.

Only Jackson seemed to maintain his balance, and hers, catching her before she toppled to the floor. "Whoa now," he rumbled, hauling her into his chest.

On instinct, she batted at his hands. The talent didn't get to touch her—ever.

He clamped her closer, smushing her nose into his broad chest so she was forced to grab onto rock hard abs to steady herself. She ended up with a big whiff of what she thought was cedarwood and lime, with a touch of underlying hot man. Before she could help herself, she'd taken a second lungful and mentally confirmed that if it wasn't lime, it was some sort of tangy citrus. Sugar had a thing for smells, both good and bad, making her susceptible to headaches and judging men by their scent. Without conscious thought, her brain declared that Jackson Wright smelled yummy.

Mentally she shook free of his spell, unnerved that she'd been so easily captivated. Firmly, she reminded herself she wasn't here to sniff the talent.

"Unhand me," she said in her iciest Wrangler voice.

He immediately set her aside, balancing her when she threatened to topple again. "My apologies. I was trying to keep you upright."

She narrowed her eyes at his clipped tone, but really, he probably had been trying to do just that. She fought the urge to argue anyway, because… well, she didn't know why, except that he annoyed her on a basic level.

"That wasn't a good sign," Russ said from where he stood forgotten beside them.

No, it wasn't. Enjoying the way Jackson smelled was bound to cause issues.

Then she realized Russ was talking about the fact the elevator had jolted to a start instead of her olfactory infatuation with the Bachelor.

Still, her small, but immediate fascination was a warning she planned to heed because she wasn't messing up this job. This was her big chance to leapfrog onto the next step on the career ladder. Lynette, the usual Head Wrangler on Hank Carson's sets, had terrible morning sickness after a surprise pregnancy and couldn't come at the last minute. Sugar wasn't going to jack up her chance at a major resume stuff because of some weird attraction. How many people working in the TV industry had ended their careers because they couldn't keep their libido in check? A million. *She* wasn't that stupid.

Determined to instill boundaries, Sugar turned to the window, trying to enjoy the view. The elevator came out of the protected shaft and into the park itself, revealing Atlantis in all its glory.

Beside her, Jackson Wright towered over her, impossible to ignore. Of course, at 5'2" everyone towered over her. A tall girl friend had once told her she should only date short guys and leave the tall ones for women who didn't have that choice, but Sugar had always found tall men attractive. She liked that feeling of being dainty, since she had a curvy figure that always made her feel bigger than she really was. Men liked T&A, and some big men like their women short, so her dating life had been active, boarding on frantic. Because while Sugar believed in love, her past taught her she probably wouldn't find it. After having her heart broken years ago, it turned out she just didn't have the ability to trust, no matter how hard she tried. Every man she'd seriously considered had disappointed her in the end.

The amusement park came fully into view in all its shadowed glory.

"Awesome," Russ said, elbowing her aside to get some footage with the handheld camera he never went anywhere without. In the distance, a small rollercoaster was visible behind a metal framed building.

She had to admit it was pretty cool in an eerie way. The sunshine from the surface filtered through the layers of water to bathe the park in a strange, ever-shifting glow. Below them, the lights were out and the rides sat motionless, but Sugar could tell this was going to be a fantastic place to film. There were tons of things to do for both group dates and one-on-ones. And the space alone would be so much easier to film in than the last two locations. Hank had managed to pull each off, despite an alien invasion on Mars and a homicidal robot on the space station, but it had been close. Logistically, those locations had been almost impossible for giving the audience the big wow moments they craved.

She was sure this location would be smooth sailing.

She and Russ had come down first to stash Jackson in his room before Hank brought the ladies who would be vying for Jackson Wright's attention later tonight. Tomorrow, Sugar had a whole list of activities they would jump into, but for tonight, the cast and crew would be settling in and having the first cocktail. Piece of cake, as long as the wardrobe made it down here. She wished there had been time to check everything before the contestants arrived, but Atlantis management had been clear that no one was allowed to arrive until today, after the park was officially closed for their maintenance window.

Beside her, Russ scanned the scene below them, completely immersed in his cameraman world as usual. "This is going to be amazing."

"Have you been here before?" Jackson asked leaning toward her, his voice like velvet across her skin.

She stifled a shiver, instead giving herself another internal lecture that Jackson was the Bachelor and not her date. It would be for the best if she nipped this instant *whatever* she had for him in the bud right now. She struggled for a moment to come up with a list of things she didn't like about him and decided he was actually too tall for her. Beside him, she felt like a Lilliputian. He was too much of a good thing in the height department, and yes, she told her libido, a guy could be too much of a good thing.

"I haven't been here, but I've reviewed videos of the location and I have mapped out all our events." Pointedly, she glanced at her clipboard, which was part of the Head Wrangler authority she wielded for her job. It was clear who she

5

was because she wore knee-high boots, jeans, and a white t-shirt that said *Bachelor Film Crew* on the front and *Head Wrangler* on the back in official black. She also signaled her crew status by wearing her hair in a disheveled ponytail, which was messy bad not messy sexy, and by her almost lack of makeup. She still had on pale lip balm and mascara because a woman had to have some pride in her appearance, but in general, the rule was the crew could never outshine the cast. It took a lot of self-confidence to be on international TV and the last thing they needed was a competition starting between the crew and the cast that might damage fragile egos.

"What exactly does a Wrangler do?" he asked, even though he could see she was busy flipping through the pages on her clipboard, which, combined with her snippy tone earlier, should have indicated to him she wasn't in the mood to talk.

She gave him what Lynette called her Sugar Stare, the one that said *don't fuck with me, I'm not putting up with it for a nanosecond.* "I keep everyone, including you, in line."

A slow, sexy smile bloomed across his face, taking his average handsome looks to the level of knockout when a dimple appeared in his right cheek. "Do I need to be kept in line?" he asked, so flirty, her internal radar began to whoop.

Time to shut him (and her own libido) down with an iron fist. "Listen, I don't know what game you're playing, but I am the only woman on this show you can't have, so please holster the dimple and can the flirtatious manner. You'll have plenty of time to bring out the big guns tonight at our first mixer when you meet the contestants."

Jackson's eyebrows crawled up his forehead in what she thought might be real surprise. "Yes, ma'am." He turned back to the view and somehow shut her out as completely as if he'd closed a door.

It was as if she'd hurt his feelings, which was strange, since the Bachelor knew what he was here for and it wasn't her.

Finally, the awkward silence was broken when the elevator reached the bottom, where it bounced twice before it made a loud slapping noise and the engine unceremoniously silenced. Sugar managed to grab the handrail, but Jackson had to steady Russ. She noticed he didn't pull the cameraman into his chest like he had her, though. She squashed the sneaking suspicion he was generally a good guy and he wasn't just playing a game with her.

"That didn't sound good," Jackson observed.

"Yeah," she said, but the doors opened so the three of them exited into the loading bay at the back of Willie's Ragtime Theater.

The cast and crew were staying in two buildings down the street where staff usually bunked when the park was open. One building would house the contestants and the other would have the Bachelor and the film crew. They would be assisted by a couple of park employees, who would help them turn the amusements on and off.

The Bachelor had to come down first so he wouldn't accidentally bump into the rest of the cast, spoiling any of the initial interactions he and the contestants might have and giving the lucky ones an advantage in the game. Time with the Bachelor equated to staying in the game. The less time a woman spent with him, the worse off she would be during the rose ceremony.

Something moved in the darkness and Sugar's heart leapt into her throat, causing her to stumble backwards into Jackson, who righted her again in that annoyingly chivalrous way she was beginning to think was part of him. This time she didn't ask him to unhand her, but instead felt comforted.

"I'm Niles Mortinson," someone said from the shadows. "I've been told to take you to your lodging." The man's voice was rusty and oddly deep. When he stepped forward, he turned out to be in his sixties, tall, extra thin and dressed completely in black, which had blended him into the darkness.

Sugar cleared the fear from her throat and stepped

forward even though she wanted to hide behind Jackson. However, because she wasn't a coward, she threw back her shoulders and faked not being afraid. "I'm Sugar, the show's Head Wrangler. This is Russ, who is in charge of filming." She waved a hand at Russ, who was, of course, filming them. Before she could introduce the Bachelor, Niles turned and shuffled away.

"Weird," Russ said, but not like she would have said it. More like he thought it was part of the cool experience.

While she stood there in surprise, Niles disappeared. She had to rush forward, tangling in the two heavy curtains that led to the theater stage before she found where they parted and was able to see Niles again. He was halfway up the aisle before they caught him. For an old guy, he could really move.

"This way," Niles said and lumbered off through the theater door and straight down the road into the semi-darkness. From the elevator, it had looked much lighter than it really was.

Luckily, Sugar had anticipated the dimness and clicked on her flashlight. She consulted the map on her clipboard to orient herself. Since the show would be paying the electric bill for the time they were here, they wouldn't use unnecessary lights until they absolutely needed them. She wanted to get her bearings before the rest of the cast arrived.

"Sugar," Russ said from beside her. "We're being left in the dust again."

Even though he was moving slowly, Niles had managed to put fifty feet between them. It was as if every time she glanced away, he ported into the near distance. She hurried to follow. Jackson fell easily in stride next to her. It took more effort than she'd like, but she managed to ignore him. She was, after all, the quintessential professional.

Behind them, Russ rambled along, probably filming everything even though they were in relative darkness.

They made their way to the end of the small street that

contained the theater and turned left on what according to her map should be International Street. Unlike the rest of the park which was filled with games and rides, this street had only shops and food stalls, which fronted the staff housing they would be staying in.

At the very end of International Street was the landing area where the submarines discharged park goers through a tin-roofed building holding ticket stalls. When the park was open, visitors usually entered the park there. Since this was off season, there would be no submarines. They were all in dry dock on the surface undergoing their annual maintenance, except for one that was attached to a track that visitors could ride in to view the park from outside the bubble.

For filming, everyone had to come in and out of the park through one elevator. Part of the crazy logistics of this trip had been getting all their supplies here on the subs before they were dry docked, so everything had arrived weeks ago. She would have to spend a lot of time unpacking once the rest of the crew arrived and she could hand off babysitting the Bachelor to someone else.

Everyone's personal luggage, which she had carefully marked, should have already been delivered to the apartments along with all the formal attire on hanging racks, unless something had gone wrong, which she desperately hoped wasn't the case. Wardrobe was everything.

"We'll be staying upstairs from Phineas' Funnel Cakes," she said, wishing she could stop to study her map to make sure. She flashed her light up to the nearest building, which said Morty's Magical Knick-Knacks trying to orient their location to the map as Niles drifted forward. They seemed to be in a shadow of some sort. It was only eight in the morning, so maybe as the sun climbed, things would lighten down here. "On the left in two blocks," she guessed, resisting the urge to glance at her clipboard.

They shambled by other shops and eateries, past the closed ice cream and hot dog stands and the Last Minute

Quick Shop. The air was slightly stale, but still hinted at cotton candy and fried food. But even with nothing open, Sugar could feel a low hum of excitement in the air, the fun just waiting to be unleashed. She loved amusement parks, as a child going with her family and anyone else she could convince to take her. She had a decent throwing arm, so she'd always won at least one stuffed animal, could drive bumper cars with the best of them, and let's face it, roller coasters rocked.

Finally, Niles turned to the left, taking out a massive ring of keys from his pocket, as he swerved around the entrance for Phineas' Funnel Cakes to an unassuming door off to the left with a small sign that said Employees Only.

They entered a short hall that led to a steep set of stairs, the old man now so slow as he climbed, Sugar had a moment to wonder why the park would send him instead someone younger. Surely Niles wasn't going to be their main contact during the filming?

"Um, Niles?" she said as they finally crested the steep stairs onto the landing.

Niles turned his whole body instead of just his head with a couple shuffle steps.

"I had thought we'd be met by someone named Barbara?"

"Barbara is busy now." He opened the single door with a massive hand and waved them inside. "I will unlock the other apartments across the street."

She had no choice but to go forward, Russ and Jackson trailing her.

But instead of following them, Niles shut the door, engulfing them in darkness.

"Did anyone else find that weird?" Jackson asked from the darkness, ending up right beside her, so close they could touch with just a shift of their weight.

Sugar stepped away and brought back out her flashlight from her messenger bag, clicking it on.

"Oh yeah," Russ said with relish. "Totally bizarre."

"What's up with Uncle Fester?" Jackson asked.

"I think you mean Lurch," Russ corrected. "He was the tall skinny butler dude."

"Him too."

"We should have been met by Barbara, who sounded very normal on the phone." Although Sugar hadn't met her in person. For a moment, she pictured Barbara as a willow thin Morticia Adams, then she shook off the thought and hit the light switch. The hallway flooded with light. Sugar realized she'd had the vague worry that the lights might not come on, but that had only been her overactive imagination at work. She reminded herself this wasn't a horror movie but a reality TV show. It had just felt like it when Niles had arrived in the shadows like that, throwing her off her game. "Let's do a quick tour up here to assign Jackson a room. He'll need one with a private bathroom," she said, moving on to her agenda. She had a ton to do tonight before the cocktail party. "We need to get the cameras set up in the apartments and tonight's location after we check on the clothes to make sure everything made it."

The two men trailed her down the hall as she flipped on the lights at every doorway, until they found a large room with a small kitchenette to the left and a lounge area filled with sofas on the right. In the middle was a huge stack of luggage in a massive, disorganized mound. Instead of putting the contestant's bags in the other building as they'd been instructed, they'd put everything in the staff and bachelor apartments.

"Uh oh," Russ said. "Someone screwed the pooch."

Sugar stuffed down the spark of annoyance, debating her options. She would either have to move all this over to the other building herself or the contestants could come get their own bags. It was a no brainer to decide on the latter. She'd stash the Bachelor behind a closed door down the hall, then bring the ladies over to get their stuff. "Grab your luggage while I go see where the hanging clothes ended up," she ordered, sinking into Head Wrangler mode. These were the types of snafus she excelled at. She was in her element, raring to problem solve and kick ass.

"Wait," Jackson said, stopping her. "Should we split up?"

She paused, surprised her first thought had been *hell no*. It would be inefficient to take them with her to find the hanging clothes, but on the other hand, this place was vaguely creeping her out.

"Here it is." Russ pulled a beat-up, massive backpack from the bottom of the stack, toppling the precariously balanced luggage with a clatter. "This has all my wiring gear in it so I can start setting up the cameras."

"I think I should go with you, just in case," Jackson said to her, his tone reasonable.

Obviously, she wasn't the only one who had a bad feeling, but she didn't like the thought of being one-on-one with the Bachelor. Although, they would be alone a lot during filming so she'd better get used to it.

From somewhere outside, a loud twang of a wire being drawn tight reverberated in the street, as if someone had released a giant arrow from a bow. The eerie sound tipped her away from her good sense. "Yeah, why don't you come with me."

CHAPTER TWO

hy are the lights all out?" Jackson asked. He figured the show wouldn't keep them in the dark the whole time, but it made what was probably a normal fun park spooky. The water above them filtered light into a mosaic of ever-changing bluish murk.

"We're paying the electric bill for the park while we're here, starting the second we entered the elevator. We'll have lights once the filming begins." Sugar led the way across the empty street to yet another door marked Employees Only. "Oh good," she said as the doorknob turned easily in her hand.

"Worried Niles didn't unlock it?" Jackson tried, and failed, to give her the space she'd clearly signaled she'd wanted.

"Let's just say Niles didn't inspire my confidence." She started up the stairs, her very nice butt cupped lovingly in jeans, the high heeled boots making her hips shift attractively with every step. "Our first cocktail will be at Ethel's Speakeasy bar. I've been told the staff will have everything set up for us by six."

"Great," he whispered, annoyed even though he had no one to blame but himself for the fact he was here.

She must have heard him, because she stopped. "You aren't excited about the first mixer?"

"Not exactly." Last week, he'd realized he'd made a

big mistake coming on the show. He'd been watching the bi-ography reel of all the contestants Hank Carson had sent him so Jackson could get to know all the ladies' names and back-grounds. He'd gotten halfway through the twelve women and, while every single one of them was gorgeous and well spoken, he'd found the videos turned him off. The worst part was he couldn't really put his finger on why. Watching those videos, he found himself nitpicking women who were, on the surface at least, perfect in every way. They were smart and beautiful, with fantastic careers and amazing volunteer work to give back to their communities.

He'd filled out a preference sheet months ago and Hank had done a great job going after his likes while avoiding his dislikes. Several of the contestants were scientists of some sort or other professionals. There was even an engineer. And there didn't seem to be any women who'd had the copious amounts of plastic surgery that made them appear like dolls, a look that he personally found a major turn-off. Jackson had always liked a natural look, and most of the contestants fell into those lines.

Maybe it was that they were all too perfect.

Sugar resumed her climb up the stairs, and as he once again appreciated her ass, he decided he preferred women who were more girl-next-door than hot model. In fact, from the moment they'd stepped on the elevator together, he'd found himself attracted to the Head Wrangler. It was almost as if her difference from the perfectness of the contestants was what drew him most. He suspected Sugar hadn't even bothered to completely brush her hair before she'd tossed it up in a ponytail and her makeup was non-existent.

His number one request had been confidence in a woman, but he'd realized watching Lena—a black-haired, green-eyed beauty from California—talk about her success that perhaps what he'd really meant was he didn't want a timid woman. Because Lena's assurance went beyond self-confi-dence and into ball busting. Jackson didn't count himself as someone who was easily frightened, but he wouldn't want to meet Lena in a dark alley.

"Every bachelor I've worked with has had nerves before filming starts." She walked into a matching hallway to the one across the street and ran her flashlight into the first room, which was empty except for two twin beds and two dressers. "Out of curiosity, why did you come on the show?"

"The money." No use trying to hide it.

Sugar gave him a look of disappointment he could feel even in the semi-darkness. He knew it was mercenary of him, but he'd put his whole life savings into the space station he'd bought with Milton and since the station no longer functioned, he knew no one in their right mind would ever buy him out of his share. It was, for all intents and purposes, a very expensive piece of floating space trash. If he was going to start over, he'd need money and Hank's offer had been too much to refuse. And by starting over, he meant buying into another space station project. After filming Atlantis Bachelor, he would have exactly the buy-in to join Project Orion. It had been as if Hank Carson had lured him by offering him the exact amount.

"Well, money can be a reason, I suppose." She flashed her light around another room.

"Why do most people become the Bachelor?" he asked, curious what it could be if it wasn't the money.

"Love," she said absently, without a hint a sarcasm or judgement.

"I see." Well, he wanted love someday. He wasn't against it, he just never seemed to have the time most women wanted from a partner.

"What are you planning on doing with the cash?" she asked, moving along the rooms.

"I'm going to buy into another space station project."

"What?" She stopped and he had to do a two-step to keep from plowing over her. "You're going to space again?"

"As soon as possible." He didn't care if he had to beg,

borrow, steal, or prostrate himself to the God of Love, he was going back.

"Why would you even want to?" she asked, in the same tone someone might ask, "why are you eating that poop sandwich?"

"Because being in space is amazing." He couldn't help but wax poetic about his first and only love. "Waking up and looking out at the vast expanse of stars surrounding you, dealing with the challenges of living in space, going where few people have ever gone. It's mind blowing."

"I would think you'd had enough after what happened last time."

"I'll never have enough of space." He winced at the drama of that statement. He wasn't a dramatic person in any way, but really who wouldn't be thrilled to live with a front row seat to the stars? "Besides, I'm not going into the hotel business again. That's where everything fell apart. This time, we'll be running a research station where different governments will rent out space." Regular tourists were too flakey to be reliable. He was going with the sure thing of government money.

"If you're going to space again soon, what are you planning to do with your fiancé?"

He paused, taken off guard since he hadn't really thought of it. She had a point, since he had a contractual agreement that he would be with the woman he proposed to for 365 days. "She can go with me," he said, feeling inspired. Because if he found love, so much the better.

He'd spent three years on the Space Station Genesis III, morphing it into a hotel in space, and while he hadn't thought about it at the time, he'd been pretty lonely. He wasn't a romantic, but the thought of having someone to snuggle up to every night held more and more appeal as he got older.

He wasn't naturally a monk. In fact, he loved women. He just loved space so much more.

"Have you considered that these women, who are all very focused on fame, don't want to go to space?" She shook her head. "There is no Instagram when you leave Earth."

"Instagram?" he asked. Why would they want to waste time on social media?

"Thank God," Sugar said, as they reached a lounge area which held several sofas and four racks of hanging dresses. She ran her hands along the tops of the hangers, shining her light on pieces of paper attached to the top of each. "They made it in one piece."

"When does everyone get here?" he asked, more to change the subject away from his love life than anything else. Sugar's questions were making him feel uneasy and he wasn't in the mood to second guess his plan.

She looked at her watch. "Dammit, time is getting away from me. We only have ten minutes until the first group arrives." She sped up her search for something hanging on the racks.

He leaned against the doorway, watching her, liking her small, but generous body. He was pretty sure he could hold her up while they had sex against a wall, something he'd always secretly wanted to try. He winced. *That* was a thought from left field.

Stop, he told himself. She'd made it clear she had no interest in him. He would soon have plenty of other choices. Why, after years of barely noticing women, was he stuck on the Head Wrangler?

She flipped through one section of hangers. "Right now, we're going to take your hanging clothes across the street and get you squared away in your room so I can go meet the first set of women coming down on the elevator." She grabbed a big section of hangers and handed them off to him, then grabbed another set and retraced their steps along the hall at a fast clip.

Then she was out of the apartments, down the steps and across the street, while he hastened to catch up. They were through the bottom door of the crew apartments when a loud BANG came from their left, making them both freeze.

"What was that?" Sugar asked.

"It came from the direction of the theater." He shifted back to the front stoop. "Think something has gone wrong with the elevator? It made that loud bang when it reached the bottom floor when we arrived." Although this sound had been much, much louder.

"Damn, maybe they're early." She hung his clothes on a sconce just inside the door and yelled at the top of the stairs, "Russ, we have to go."

There was no answer.

"Russ," she called again.

Silence.

Sugar let out an adorable growl. "He's probably in his own world wiring something. Can you go up and send him to the theater? If the women are here, you need to be in your room sooner than we'd anticipated. You can't meet anyone early. That's against the rules."

"Sure," he said, fighting a mild sadness that his time before the show was over. He'd made his bed and he had to lie in it. The dye was cast and his future was now spinning forward out of control.

She was gone in a flash, taking her big personality and pleasant company with her.

Jackson had no choice but to haul his armload of clothing up the stairs. He hung them in the closet of his assigned room and wandered along the hall looking for Russ, who was nowhere to be found. Maybe he'd already gone to the elevator. Or had wandered off to film something.

Jackson went back for the other armload of clothes, wondering when he'd have time to wear them all and why he needed multiple tuxes when one tux was more than enough.

From far away, a scream filled the air.

Forgetting Sugar's warning to stay in his room, he raced out into the street, trying to figure out where the oddly distorted sound had come from. Guessing, he ran toward the theater.

———

Sugar heard the scream as she entered the theater and stumbled through the curtain toward it, instead of turning around and running the other way, which was secretly what she wanted to do. She was the Head Wrangler on this show, she reminded herself. Head Wranglers ran toward danger, not away from it.

She entered to find a room in chaos. People moved in the darkness, with crying, squeals and moans filling the air. She ran her flashlight across the tableau, struggling to make sense of what she saw, bodies twisting and stooping, one person appearing to drag another.

"What's going on?" she asked in her loudest, Head Wrangler voice.

"The elevator," a woman cried and Sugar illuminated her with her flashlight to find Lena, blood streaming down her beautiful face.

Sugar scanned the elevator, seeing that it was no longer fully sitting inside the shaft, but tilted half into the room. "Is everyone out?"

She crossed through the women who had pulled themselves into loading bay and crouched down to shine the light inside the car. No one was still inside, thank God.

She stood, her mind stumbling on what to do.

Lynette had once told her that when in doubt about how to handle something, fake it. She was in charge. She needed to stop the chaos immediately.

First things first, fuck the light bill. She trailed the flashlight along the wall until she found the switch and flipped it on.

"Okay," she said loudly and with authority, blinking through the sudden brightness. She knew they were sending the contestants in batches of four or five, since the elevator was small. Hank would bring up the rear with the last set, Cindy would be in the first, so Cindy had to be here somewhere.

She scanned the five women until she located the Assistant Wrangler on this shoot. "Cindy, are you okay?" she asked, kneeling beside her.

"Something is wrong with my leg," Cindy said, cradling the top of her thigh in both hands.

It looked like a normal leg to Sugar, but she'd really only half paid attention to the required first aid class they'd had to take. "How bad is it?

Cindy winced in pain. "Bad. I can't put any weight on it and my knee feels like it's been twisted."

Damn, that wasn't good. "Can you hang tight while I check on the others?"

"I'll be fine. Go." Cindy was a fantastic Assistant Wrangler and professional enough not to add to Sugar's burdens. They'd worked on several previous shows together.

Sugar scanned the room, finding Andi, Lena, Raven and Jillian huddled on the floor. She started with the one closest. "Lena, are you okay?"

Lena was crying in a huddle ball, still managing to look beautiful and fragile, with her black hair and large green eyes shimmering with tears. "I hit my head. I'm bleeding," she said, revealing a cut on her forehead about half an inch long. Not too big but it was bleeding badly.

Sugar resisted the urge to pull back. Command, she reminded herself, scanning around wondering where the hell Russ was. "Put your hand on it and apply pressure," she ordered.

"Here," Cindy said, offering Sugar a stack of napkins she had from god only knew where.

"Hold pressure," she ordered transferring the stack of white squares, hearing Russ arrive behind her. "Russ, I need the first aid kit. Now," she said without turning.

"I couldn't find him," Jackson said. "I'll be right back with it." And he was gone before she could tell him he was breaking the rules and order him to get his ass back to his room.

"Jillian what's wrong?" she asked, moving on to where the blonde-haired woman was sitting with Andi.

"Nothing but bruises for me, but Andi's got a pretty bad cut on her arm." Jillian had taken off her sweater and wrapped it around the other woman's arm.

"Keep holding pressure." Pressure, she vaguely remembered, was the answer to all emergencies involving blood. "Let me check on Raven." Sugar figured at this point, she needed to understand what had happened to everyone.

Raven slouched against the wall, looking like she'd fainted.

"Raven," Sugar said, first shaking her shoulder and then giving her a tap on the cheek.

No response.

She shook Raven's shoulder harder and the girl moaned. She was alive. That was good, and she didn't seem to be bleeding anywhere. "What's wrong? Are you hurt?"

Raven moaned again. Out of everyone, Raven seemed to be the worst off. One thing was for certain, they all needed immediate, professional attention.

It suddenly hit Sugar like a ton of bricks that with the elevator out of service and the submarines dry docked, there was no way to get help here.

Oh crap! I'm in serious trouble.

She was all on her own.

CHAPTER THREE

*J*ackson had made a large tactical error when he forgot to ask Sugar where the first aid kit was stored. He spent about ten minutes tossing aside suitcases in the crew apartments when he realized this was only the cast's luggage, every piece carefully labeled with someone's name. He sat back on his heels and tried to imagine where the support supplies might be kept and came up blank. There was probably a filming headquarters nearby with all their equipment, but the street was filled with store fronts hiding offices and apartments so there was no use randomly looking. The park was huge and he didn't have time to roam around, trying doorknobs.

Then it struck him that maybe the kitchen behind him had one. He pivoted to check, figuring if this didn't bear fruit, he'd go across the street.

He scanned the kitchenette, reading the labels on each cabinet until he found FIRST AID KIT. Grabbing the large black tackle box, he hustled from the room, reviewing the pandemonium in the theater in his mind. Impressing him to no end, Sugar had been singlehandedly handling the situation when he'd arrived. If someone had been seriously hurt, Sugar would have asked for assistance instead of sending him for the first aid kit, but at least one person had been bleeding.

He knew time was of the essence for him to get back there and help out, so he picked up the pace, hoofing it down on the street, huffing and puffing at a sort-of run. His cardio had gone to hell up on Genesis III. It wasn't like he could go for a jog in space.

Although… he could rig something up, maybe a stationary bike of some kind.

He'd managed to maintain his weight lifting by using resistance bands and anything heavy he could find. Plus pushups. Lots and lots of pushups and crunches. He'd always been someone who enjoyed working out, taking his body to the limits, but the fact was, nothing brought him more joy than going up in space. After all, nothing pushed him further and challenged him more than living in the sky.

He distracted himself from the pain of the run, which had turned into more of a shuffle as he neared the theater, by going over the list of everything he'd need to bring for a cardio workout next time he went into space. His luggage weight was always capped, so he'd have to be smart about it.

When he finally burst through the curtain in the theater, he found Sugar helping a woman propped against the wall.

"I have it," he said, kneeling beside her.

"Help Andi first," she ordered, pointing to two women huddled across the room.

He tried to remember if Andi was the redhead or the blonde as he scooched over. "Andi?" he asked to them generally, since he was drawing a blank.

"Me," said the one laying down. The redhead. From Spokane. Veterinarian who rescued horses off the track.

"She's got a big cut," said the blonde, who was holding a piece of clothing to the other woman's arm.

He unzipped the first aid case and saw various gauze and medical pads, and some vials and pill bottles. A quick scan had him pulling out a thick pad, opening the packaging and positioning it over her arm. "Let's see what's happening under there. When I say go, pull away the sweater and I'll put on this pad. Ready?"

"Yes."

"Go." They switched positions and he got a quick glimpse at a three-inch cut down Andi's arm. Stitches were needed for sure, but already the bleeding had slowed to more of a seep, which was a good sign.

Andi saw it too and moaned.

"What's your name?" he asked the blonde.

"Jillian." She blinked, big blue eyes going wide. "Oh, you're the Bachelor."

"Yeah," he said, wishing he wasn't. "Are you okay?" He gave her a quick once over but she appeared fine. Better than fine, really. Tall and thin, with obvious self-confidence and the common sense to improvise in a crisis. Sadly, he felt nothing but antsy to get away to see where else he could help.

"I'm more than okay," she said, then grinned and gave him a wink.

"Great," he said, ignoring the flirtation. "Take over holding pressure and I'll go check on the other woman. I'll be back."

"I'll be here," she answered in a sing-song.

He left quickly. "Are you okay?" he asked Lena, because he remembered her from the videos.

"Yeah. My head is killing me, though." She brought away a stack of napkins and he saw the half-inch long cut still trickling blood.

"Here," he said, finding a couple 4x4 gauze pads in the kit and handing them to her. "Put more pressure to stop the bleeding and we'll apply antiseptic and butterfly bandages on it after it stops." He'd taken an advanced first aid and CPR class before he'd left for Genesis III, since he'd been worried about Milton's heart. Milton had been a great guy to partner with, since he was fantastic at handling the guests, but he was a man who enjoyed enormous steaks and single malt scotch. Years of fine living had taken its toll.

"Thanks," she said. "My head is pounding."

She didn't seem to notice he was the Bachelor yet.

Probably because he'd cut his hair, something he'd done when his sister had texted him a picture of himself looking like Fabio walking out of a train tunnel with lights surrounding him. It had been ridiculous and his family had gotten a great kick out of it—to the point it had become a running joke that would never end. One that had begun to annoy him, especially after Cassie had added music, a hammer and a cape, with the words *I must go back to Asgard, but I give you my word I will return for you* across the bottom. He assumed that was some sort of Thor reference based on the responses of his two brothers, who found it hilarious.

While he loved his family, they had always thought he was too serious. This whole Bachelor thing had made the Wright clan giddy with the opportunity to tease him. When he'd agreed to Hank's proposal, all he'd thought about was getting back into space, not the impact to other parts of his life.

The bottle marked "Aspirin" was empty. "I have some pain relievers in my bag I can get you." He'd need to run back for them, but that wasn't the end of the world. He could work on his cardio. There was no time like the present to get in shape.

Her eyes scrunched up in obvious pain. "I think I'm going to need them," she said, her tone full of wry humor, softer than the ball buster on her video.

In fact, in person he found her to be sweet, which was weird, because it had been her video that had been such a large turn off. "I'll be back to check on you." He made his way to the older woman propped against the wall right beside the elevator, wracking his brain for her name. "Do you need help?"

"I'm Cindy," she said, saving him from embarrassing himself. "My knee is blowing up like a balloon. Can you help with that?" About fifty years old, Cindy wore her hair in a bob that was just kissing into gray. He vaguely remembered that she was one of the staff members they'd listed on his never-ending paperwork.

He studied the knee, which was double the size of her other one, and winced. "That is certainly swollen. Is your leg broken? Or is it just the knee?" Not that the knee wasn't bad enough. On the bright side, she didn't seem to have a compound fracture.

"I don't think anything is broken."

"That's a relief." He resisted the urge to feel along her leg to make sure. He would leave that to the professionals. Speaking of which, where were they?

"If I sit still, it doesn't even hurt, so go work on making the others more comfortable."

"This bag didn't have any pain relievers, but you'll be the first person I bring some to," he promised, grabbing his kit to stand.

It was really the first time he could take a good look around him. The elevator half leaned into the room, it's cables obviously broken, the protective steel doors smashed. They were all lucky to be alive. The banging noise from when he and Sugar had ridden in it earlier must have been a cable breaking. This was a catastrophe, but a small, secret part of him saw a silver lining since obviously the show couldn't film now that this had happened. Relief spilled over him, until he remembered he needed the show to get back into space.

Without money, he'd be stuck on Earth. The thought sliced through him like knife. He'd had everything he'd ever wanted on Genesis III. It might have been old, but he was the best space engineer in the business and he'd systematically fixed each system until it had been in perfect working order. If Alphie hadn't gone insane, he would still be up there, doing what he did best.

Still, he wasn't dead yet. If he was breathing, he would have hope. He'd found a way up once, he would find a way again. Besides, this gig was a bird in the hand. As long as he fulfilled his part of the deal, they'd have to pay him. Maybe. He'd have to check the contract.

If they did end up filming, he'd have to choose one of the contestants, but the only woman he seemed to have interest so far in was Sugar, who was strictly off limits.

Maybe he could talk Hank into making Sugar one of the contestants? He'd choose her without a moment's hesitation. Then he realized it was Sugar's very difference that attracted him in the first place. And besides, he couldn't imagine her wanting to dress up in slinky formal attire. He stared across the room, trying to picture her in heels and a tight dress, but came up blank. She was a woman who would be best in jeans and a flannel shirt, curled up beside him on the couch in front of a fire on a winter's day.

Wow, that was a specific fantasy. One he'd never had before in his life. There weren't fires in space. Jackson wondered what the hell was wrong with him. Maybe there was something wacky in the air down here.

"When is help arriving?" Cindy whispered, obviously trying not to alert the others.

"Let me powwow with Sugar for a second," he said, and crossed to her for an ETA.

Sugar's patient was moaning and disoriented. "What happened?" she asked.

"The elevator crashed and you hit your head," Sugar replied in a tone which said this wasn't new territory. "Do you remember?"

"No," the woman answered.

Uh oh. Jackson figured this wasn't the right time to be asking too many questions about help arriving, since no one would be using the elevator again today. Or tomorrow. He looked at the listing hulk of ruined metal, knowing instinctively that Humpty Dumpty wasn't going to be put back together again, maybe ever. Still, Atlantis had to have some other backup way to get people down to help them. A freight elevator or something. In fact, he'd have thought help would be here already. "Do you know where the show's first aid kit is?" he asked.

"You don't have it?"

"I grabbed one from our apartments but it doesn't have any pain killers."

"Damn. I bet it's with the rest of our equipment." Sugar frowned and he had an odd desire to try to comfort her.

"Where? I'll get it."

She shook her head. "It's all the way down at the Catering Pavilion. We were supposed to be issued golf carts for the duration. Niles disappeared before I could ask him about them." She looked around, slightly desperate. "Speaking of Niles, where is he? The sound of the elevator crashing should have woken the dead." Her eyes narrowed. "And where the hell is Russ? He better not be off filming plastic bags floating in the wind or some crap."

"Um, Sugar, we are in a bubble under the water. There is no wind here." He wondered if she was having some sort of shock reaction and resisted the urge to touch her brow.

She waved a hand. "Old film reference. If I know Russ, and I do, he's goofing around. I'm going to shoot him when he finally shows up."

"I didn't see him at the apartments." Although he hadn't been looking too closely. Russ could have been across the street setting up cameras, oblivious to them needing him.

"He's probably filming a sea turtle swimming on the other side of the bubble or getting b-roll to put in his blooper video. He's a dead man walking when he finally shows up," she promised and he believed her. "Jillian, can you sit with Raven?"

With a word to Andi, Jillian handed off the duty of holding pressure and came over.

"She's got a concussion. Just keep explaining to her over and over what happened when she forgets. Jackson and I are going to find the show's first aid kit and some water. I'm putting you in charge, since Cindy is hurt so badly. Just ask Cindy if you aren't sure what to do."

"You've got it," Jillian said, taking Sugar's place.

Jackson remembered that he was here to find his soul-mate, so he admitted he liked Jillian's no-nonsense demeanor. It would be a great asset in space, but then again, a veterinar-ian wouldn't want to leave her practice. Although, wait, that was Andi's job...

He tried to remember what Jillian did for a living, but came up blank. He was supposed to know all this already, but he found he was having trouble accessing the files in his brain. Or maybe he had been so focused on the fact he'd made a major mistake coming on the show that he hadn't been paying attention.

Well, it was too late now. He'd made his bed and would have to lie in it.

He offered Sugar a hand to help her up and after a moment, she took it and he pulled her easily to her feet since she was so tiny. He'd always thought good things came in little packages, and Sugar had a lot of good things to her.

Sugar is not an option. Stop focusing on her.

"Jackson, you're with me." Sugar lead the way out at a fast clip, assuming he would follow, which he did.

"I could go without you," he offered, hustling to catch up. She might be short, but she was fast.

"You wouldn't know where it is and I can't leave you alone with the contestants."

"What?" Wait, was she still playing the game? "I thought an elevator crash would mean the end of the show?"

"Until Hank Carson says so, this show is a go." She set off at a bit of a jog so he had to as well. "Haven't you ever heard the phrase *the show must go on?*" Her tone was amused and light, as if she were energized by the current crisis.

"How can we possibly still go through with this after they all almost died?" Although he thought one of his sisters said something about contestants really dying on Mars, so maybe death on one of these shows wasn't unusual. Or had Cassie been speaking metaphorically? With his sister, you never knew.

"You're missing the crucial word in that sentence."

"What word is that?"

"Almost," she said and ran ahead.

He sighed silently and followed her, bummed there would be more running and even more that the show was going to go on. Now that it was out of his hands, he wished it was cancelled. *The money,* he reminded himself. *Space.* He could do this. He *would* do this.

"Where's our rescue?"

"I'm pretty sure it's going to be awhile before they get someone down here."

A bad feeling crawled up his spine. "There isn't a backup elevator?"

"Nope. Which means we have to plan for it to take time for help to arrive."

Jackson had so many questions but instead he concentrated on keeping up. If he could speak, he would have said that he wished she'd slow down. But instead he chugged in air as he trailed her along International Street, turning right before they got to the apartments, then down a long gradual hill to the bottom where there were several corrugated metal buildings and an outdoor amphitheater, with an old style, Southern mansion house at the end of the cul-de-sac.

To pass the time and ignore being out of shape, he reviewed the plan for securing his next space journey. Mark Warner had told him he could buy into their venture and get a twenty percent ownership with a combination buy-in and working arrangement. Jackson had much-needed expertise since he'd spent so much time in space. But even with experience, these plans wouldn't be possible without money and money wouldn't be forthcoming without playing the Bachelor. Mentally, he recommitted to playing his role, which was finding his perfect soulmate.

Although Sugar seemed to think none of the contestants would live with him at the space station, which made no sense at all. Living in space was one of the coolest experiences anyone could have. Why wouldn't they jump at a chance to move there? Unless they had a veterinarian practice. Obviously, Andi couldn't pick up and move for the duration. He thought one of them was an attorney. That wasn't a job they could walk away from. And he supposed some people wanted to live near their families. Jackson loved his family, but they were better at a distance. At the end of every Christmas when he was Earth side, he had his own celebration once he escaped to his apartment into blessed silence.

They headed toward the largest shed at the bottom of the hill.

"Now let's see if the door is unlocked," she said, barely out of breath, grabbing the handle to door which slid sideways along the building to reveal pitch black inside. She clicked on her flashlight and ran the beam along the closest wall, looking for the light switch, which rested above rows of what appeared to be workbenches, tools on hooks above them.

With a flick of the switch, light flooded the space revealing crates of items, with BACHELOR spray painted in red along the sides, in the center of the room. To the left were nine golf carts all neatly parked in three rows. At the back of the warehouse sat a small train shaped like a whale, with an engine and three cars with space for two people each. The whale was grinning at him.

To the right was a hodgepodge of spare parts and bins of supplies he would love to explore. Jackson really was at his best when he was working with his hands fixing things. He could take the smallest item of metal trash and reuse it to salvage a system.

"There are the golf carts," he said hopefully, wishing they could ride back instead of run up the hill they'd just come down.

"Yeah. Now to find the first aid kit in all this."

They spread out, reading the helpful lists someone had stapled onto the side of each container. The crates were filled with every conceivable item, from food, to alcohol, to condoms. Which made Jackson think of sex (which was natural) with Sugar (which was not). Specifically, he imagined Sugar wrapped around him while he kissed her bare shoulder. He would love to run his mouth along the sweet curve of her neck.

No, no he wouldn't. *Get a hold of yourself, man! She's the only woman here that is off limits.*

He wondered if maybe it was the very fact she was off limits that attracted him. But no, he'd never once had pangs of desire for someone else's wife or girlfriend. He'd never once felt like he wanted to have a secret affair. He hated secrets. They always ended up eating people to pieces, destroying the very thing that they protected.

He'd only met four of the contestants so far, and they had been in the middle of a terrifying crisis. This wasn't the time to write them off. There might easily be one or two people who he had chemistry with, like he had with Sugar.

"This one," she said, completely oblivious to his internal struggles. She was obviously not thinking of him as someone special.

He found a crowbar and pried the top off. She pulled herself over the high edge and reached far down into the crate, her legs kicking out behind her.

"Need help?" he asked, watching her struggle with some amusement. Nothing seemed to keep Sugar from her goals.

"I've almost... there! Got it." She grabbed a huge pink bag from the sea of other things inside.

"Pink?" he asked.

"Hard to lose a pink bag," she said, then she pointed at a nearby crate. "Open that one and put a bunch of waters on the back of a cart. We can come back for more later."

He followed orders quickly, tempted to grab a water for himself, but then he figured he would leave a trail of bottles falling out of the cart on the way up the hill if he tore the plastic bundling them.

Sugar went to the front of the cart. "No keys."

"There's a key box," he said, finishing with the water, then going over to the black cabinet affixed to the wall. When he opened it, keys galore were revealed. For a moment, he studied the label which read *whale*, then he grabbed one of the keys below a *golf* label. "Here's one."

"You sure it fits?" she asked as he passed it to her.

"It was hanging under a label which said 'golf' and has the golf cart key shape."

"You play golf?" She seemed surprised.

"When I'm on Earth." He unplugged the cart from the charging station.

She sat on the bench seat, inserted the key and pressed the start button, but nothing happened.

"You have to push the break while pressing the button for it to start."

She did and the electric motor sprung to life.

"Voila!"

"Amazing." She grinned at him.

He ignored the fact he liked her smiling. They were co-workers. Nothing more. "Ready?"

She pursed her lips in thought. "We should take two carts up. Can you bring another one to the apartments for me?"

"As you wish," he said, grabbing another key.

"I'll take this one and go to the theater."

"I'll come with you," he said, because there was something in her tone that said she was going to split them up and his gut said they should stick together. Which was silly. The elevator had failed because of poor maintenance, not sabotage.

Maybe it was his weird attraction to her making up reasons for them to stick together. But both Niles and Russ hadn't arrived after the elevator had fallen. That sound was loud enough so everyone in Atlantis should have come running. And hadn't Niles said something about a woman named Barbara when they'd first arrived? Where was she?

"I need to go to the theater, but you're going to go to Morty's Magical Knick Knacks and break in since we can't seem to find any of the Atlantis staff to unlock the doors. In the back room there is an emergency phone to call the surface. By now Hank knows something is wrong, but we need a way to communicate with them to make sure they don't think the elevator is just stuck or temporarily jammed so they know to send help. Then if you get any extra time, you're going to drive around the park and figure out where the fuck Russ is and tell him to get his ass to the theater to help." She slid out of the cart to grab the pink bag which she'd left on the ground.

"Yes, ma'am," he said, unable to resist a grin at her bossy tone. He was so glad he wasn't Russ right now.

"Thanks for everything," she said. "You've really been a huge help." She squeezed his arm on her way by in a friendly way.

He caught her hand, turning her, his skin tingling at her touch, the pink bag bumping into his leg. For some reason, he really wanted to kiss her. He leaned closer, wondering if her lips were as soft as they seemed. This was most likely just a stress reaction, but her lips drew him almost without a choice.

For a second, their gazes met and as she swayed toward him he felt sure she wanted to kiss him, too.

Then she ruined it by adding, "We're going to get this sorted out and start filming as soon as possible to find your soulmate. Maybe we can do some interviews tonight after this settles down about what you want in a perfect partner."

She slipped free from his hold and he let her go, the moment gone as quickly as it had come.

While he stood there thinking that was the last thing he wanted to talk to her about, she stashed the pink bag on the passenger side of the cart, jumped behind the wheel and put the pedal to the metal, roaring from the warehouse—or roaring as fast as a golf cart could.

He watched her drive off, feeling rebuffed since he was pretty sure she knew he'd been about to kiss her. She was clearly the smarter person out of the two of them, able to remain a professional.

One thing he was sure of from the exchange. Sugar was a hell of a woman. And completely off limits.

CHAPTER FOUR

Sugar braked to a stop in front of the Willie's Ragtime Theater, still debating if Jackson had been about to kiss her in the warehouse.

Not Jackson, she reminded herself. The Bachelor. The man who at best was going to marry one of the contestants and at worst would end up living with them for the year he promised in his contract. He was, as far as she was concerned, basically engaged already. He just hadn't put the ring on one of the twelve fingers being offered to him.

Ergo, he wasn't available. Sugar had a strict policy never to mess with another woman's man.

Technically, he doesn't have a woman yet, a small voice in her mind pointed out.

In a few hours, he would start dating women who weren't her, and she didn't put up with that kind of shinnanery.

She grabbed the water and the pink bag, and hoofed it inside.

There could not be a man who was more of a 'no' in this universe than Jackson Wright.

She would do best to remember that. Often. Because this show was her chance to finally move ahead, and her career meant everything to her. She planned to never be assistant wrangler again. Once she had her baby, Lynette might always be head wrangler on Hank's shows, but Sugar could and would move to another series and enjoy not only the huge pay raise but also the responsibility she seemed to crave.

And she wouldn't get all those things if she ended up sleeping with the talent. That was the kiss of death.

Her job was to help love bloom between Jackson and the contestants, she reminded herself as she double timed it through the theater.

Although Jackson had said he wanted one of these women to move to space with him. She choked out a laugh as she shouldered her way through the curtains. Never going to happen. If Jackson thought these women were going to live on a space station somewhere, he was not only unrealistic, but when the women heard his plans, they were going to defect in droves. They were expecting to live for a year in a mansion in LA, with interviews and appearances and building their brands. Not in some tin can in space.

Hank should have caught this in the vetting process. She would ask him what the hell he'd been thinking, if he ever got down here where she could talk to him alone. Because this was going to be a problem. Not *her* problem, she reminded herself, and what happened after the show was the least of her worries. Right now, she had a disaster on her hands, the kind she was paid to solve.

Untangling herself from the curtain, Sugar found the room had shifted, with Jillian circling everyone around Cindy. Sugar remembered something about Jillian wanting to be a nurse growing up, but finding her true calling by becoming a social worker with adult protective services. She was obviously the right person to put in charge of everyone, since both Andi and Lena had been bandaged and Cindy had a splint on her leg.

"Wow, you've been busy," Sugar said, as she began handing out pain relievers like candy.

"Jillian is amazing," Cindy said, wincing as she moved her leg a fraction of an inch.

"I was just about to help Raven get to the bathroom,"

Jillian said, her voice brisk and efficient, unlike her playful bi-ography videos and the taped interview she'd had with Hank all the staff had watched before making the final twelve selections. They'd picked her because she came across as bouncy, upbeat and sincere.

"Thank God. I'm about to burst." Raven started to rise, but staggered. Jillian and Sugar jumped in to support her on either side to the bathroom, which was luckily right around the corner.

That crisis averted, Sugar distributed the rest of the water and pills, then went back to Cindy, who was hurt the worst and therefore her biggest concern. "I'm glad they splinted that leg."

"Yeah," Cindy said, a definite lack of excitement in her voice.

"How bad is it?"

"Not horrible," Cindy lied like a good soldier. She'd always seemed content as an assistant wrangler. Fulfilled and happy. Maybe Sugar would be happier if she just stopped climbing the ladder and found contentment where she was. The thought was so foreign, she discarded it.

Sugar had always liked Cindy, who was short, spunky, and loved changing her hair into a myriad of colors. Today it was a placid gray. Sugar thought it was a vast improvement to last week's green, which had washed her out and made her always seem to be on the edge of an illness. A Zumba instructor, Cindy had more energy than all the rest of the crew put together. She would randomly break out into choruses of "join the party!" which seemed to be some sort of Zumba slogan, with a grapevine thrown in for emphasis.

"What should our plan be?" Sugar asked, because honestly, she was feeling at a bit of a loss.

"They're going to get down here and rescue us soon, right?"

Sugar didn't bother lying. "It might be a while before they can make it if they have to come in with a submarine.

They're all in dry dock right now." She didn't know any other way with the elevator no longer working. They were lucky someone hadn't been killed when the elevator crashed. "As much as I hate to say it, I think we should plan to be here alone for a couple of days."

Cindy looked at the swelling on her knee. "That's going to suck."

"Yeah it will." Sugar didn't add that they didn't have an endless supply of painkillers in the bottle. She figured she would cross that bridge when they got to it. The park had to have a nurse's station somewhere. "Do we leave everyone here or move them to their rooms?"

"Rooms," Cindy said. "I'm the only one who can't walk, so let's get them moving and thinking about the game. We can say it's an advantage to have extra time with him."

Sugar glanced to where all the contestants were clustered together for support. "I don't like Raven's concussion."

"No, but she hasn't asked what happened since she returned from the bathroom, so that's an improvement. She will have to suck it up until they can get us out. We'll make Jillian her roommate to look after her."

"I agree. Okay, you want to go first or last?" Sugar figured since Cindy was most injured, she got to choose.

"Last. Then you can get that hunky bachelor in here to help me. Just looking at him makes me feel better." Cindy raised and lowered her eyebrows a few times, more like her old self.

"Oh, good lord," Sugar said, suppressing a laugh. Cindy was always outrageous. She stood up. "Okay ladies! We're going to move you guys to your rooms so you can relax while we work on getting a doctor down here to check everyone out. I have a golf cart in front of the theater. Why don't Jillian and Andi come with me first and then I'll come get the other two of you?"

They trooped out and after a couple quick trips, she had the four of them safely in their rooms with their bags.

With some breathing room established, she walked down to Morty's Magical Knick Knacks to see what Hank had to say and get the Bachelor so they could move Cindy.

⌣

Breaking into Morty's Magical Knick Knacks turned out to be harder than Jackson had anticipated. Rather than kick in the door, which would have been cool but also could have ended up breaking his toes, Jackson returned to the Catering Pavilion for some tools to pick the lock. He'd gone through a stage in his youth where he'd broken into every locked room in his parent's house at least once, but it had been years and he was rusty. Luckily it was like riding a bike and he was inside in a couple minutes.

Morty's was a much smaller shop than he had anticipated. While it was filled with aisles of bric-a-brac visitors could waste their hard-earned money on, the store itself was only about twenty feet wide by ten feet deep. A long counter took up the back of the store and behind it was a door marked Employees Only.

Jackson pulled up the hinged countertop to access behind the counter but the lock on the Employee's Only door was much better than the one on the door to the outside.

"Huh," he said, studying it. This would require a lot more work and a lot more skill.

He flipped on every light so he could study it, wondering at the upgrade to security. Then he set to work with his improvised picks, feeling the tumblers as he gently lifted every one by feel, only to have them all thunk back down at the last second.

He tried again. He wasn't big on giving up. There had been times on Genesis III that he had wanted to throw in the towel, especially when the gravity machine had broken and he couldn't seem to jerry rig something to get it up and running again no matter how hard he'd tried. But even in a space suit, floating around bouncing off walls like a pinball, he had been able to figure things out. A single lock wouldn't defeat him.

It took him a long time to crack it, but he did. He grinned, wishing he had someone to celebrate with. Then he flipped on the light switch, finding himself in what was obviously the command center of the park. One wall was filled with a bank of screens which showed murky pictures of the park, the security footage still rolling even though there wasn't anyone watching. In the center of the room stood a tall table with just enough space to hold an old-fashioned telephone. The moment he approached it, it rang as if someone knew he had arrived.

It made him jump sideways into a crouch. Wow, he hadn't realized how itchy this place was making him.

The phone rang again.

He straightened, feeling a little sheepish at his overreaction. "Hello?" There must be cameras somewhere in the room, but a quick scan didn't reveal any. Perhaps they were so small, he couldn't see them.

"Who is this?" a stressed, male voice demanded on the other end.

Or maybe no one had been watching. "Jackson Wright."

"Oh, oh, Jackson. This is Hank," Hank said with a long-suffering sigh.

"I was just going to call you." Jackson stared at the computer screens and noticed another golf cart had joined his outside, but no one was with it. "Sugar had me reach you while she dealt with the ladies who were hurt."

"The elevator malfunctioned?" Hank asked.

"Worse than that. Looks like one of the cables snapped."

"How many were hurt?"

"Almost all of them have an injury but Cindy's knee is severely swollen and Raven lost consciousness and seems to have a concussion. The others have minor cuts and bruises.

What's the status on getting us out?" he asked, right before someone reached around him to push the button marked *speaker*, filling the room with Hank's voice.

"Well, that's complicated," Hank said.

Jackson grinned at Sugar, feeling a little lift with her presence.

But Sugar wasn't looking at him. Instead, she stared at the phone with extra annoyance. The ponytail her hair had been in earlier sagged and she seemed a bit worse for wear, but her spirit in the face of adversity hadn't flagged one bit as she put her hands on her hips and geared up for battle. "Don't give me complicated, Hank Carson. I want an ETA," Sugar said, not standing for prevarication for even a second.

"I can't give you one. Yet," he added, speaking louder as if to head her off. "We're bringing a submarine out of dry dock, so it's going to take a little time."

"How much time?"

"Well," Hank said, hesitating.

Sugar stared at the ceiling as if for divine guidance. "Just say it."

"Earliest tomorrow night. Maybe two days from now."

"Oh. My. God," Sugar said and marched in a tight circle to blow off some anxiety. "It's Tuesday Hank. Are you saying you might not be here until Thursday? Because that's way too long."

Jackson rolled over a chair and sat down to enjoy the show. While it wasn't the best situation, he found Atlantis to be rather like space, except for the spooky atmosphere. Adversity handed you situations and you dealt with them. Personally, he found he enjoyed living like this. And he was extra enjoying watching Sugar rise to the occasion.

"I know, I know," Hank was saying and Jackson could imagine him patting the air. "But this wasn't something we could have anticipated and Thursday will be here before you know it."

"That's not true. You should have had a backup exit strategy. That's a normal contingency when dealing with dangerous locations."

"Actually, for the last three seasons, we've had limited options in terms of backup plans. When filming in these kinds of exotic locations, you have to be flexible," Hank said, sounding a little like he was reciting something he'd said a million times before. "They involve a bit of inherent risk."

"Please don't give me the party line," Sugar growled. "Because now we're in a situation and flexibility isn't going to get me squat. I've got several problems I'm dealing with here and you need to be offering solutions."

"Which contestants were hurt?"

"All but Jillian. But Cindy needs an x-ray and Raven should see a doctor at the very least. Any way you could lower ropes down to haul them out?"

"That elevator shaft seems to have collapsed half way down. By the time I find teams to dig out the debris, the sub would be there."

Sugar drummed her fingers on the table, clearly annoyed by Hank's answer. "We need someone here latest tomorrow, Hank. Think of the scandal that would occur if one of the contestants died."

"Die?" Hank asked, incredulous and worried. "Of what?"

"Raven has a concussion that could be a brain bleed. And Cindy could get blood poisoning from her injured leg."

"Blood poisoning?" Hank asked.

Jackson had to agree Sugar pushed it a bit far with that one, but he saw her point.

"We need that submarine. Tomorrow, not in two days."

"Let me see what I can do." Hank sounded extremely stressed.

"Also, Russ is missing."

"Missing?" Hank asked, incredulous.

"He's been gone since before the elevator crashed. Unless you've seen him?" she asked Jackson hopefully.

"Nope." Jackson hadn't exactly had time to look. "But I could search if you'd like. He has to be somewhere. It's not like he can leave the park."

"What do you mean missing?" Hank asked again.

Sugar flapped a hand. "He's wandered off someplace to film and must have lost track of time. But I really need him to help me here. Especially with Cindy out of commission."

"It's too close to filming for him to have wandered off." Now Hank sounded puzzled. "Russ might hyper-focus but he'd never miss an opportunity to film contestants."

"If you hadn't let them shut down cell service, I could have called him. Maybe until help arrives, the park could turn the cell service back on? Then we could talk in real time."

"I'll ask," Hank said, but grumpily, most likely because of the cost. Even popular shows had to have budgets. "Russ has to be around someplace."

"I can look for him," Jackson offered.

"I need you to help me move Cindy first."

"Of course." He grinned at her, but only got narrowed eyes in return. Jackson didn't take it personally. This was a total clusterfuck for sure.

"Maybe you could do some contestant interviews," Hank suggested.

Sugar frowned. "With Cindy out of commission and Russ MIA, I'm really stretched thin right now. I feel like I'm holding things together with my fingernails. If Jackson hadn't been able to step in to help, I would really be in trouble."

"This isn't like Russ. Are you sure he isn't off setting up cameras? Where was your first event supposed to be?"

"Ethel's Speakeasy. We haven't had time to check so I guess he could be there. Jackson can you check it out?"

Jackson nodded. He'd do anything if it kept him out of his room.

"Let's talk again in two hours." She looked at her

watch. "1pm?"

Jackson was surprised at how much time had passed. He'd been officially on the show for three hours now, but it felt like days.

"1pm. Lynette is here and wants to say something to you."

"Hey Sugar," Lynette said and Jackson could picture the brown haired, brown eyed spitfire in his mind. "I'm so sorry to leave you in this mess."

"You can't help that your morning sickness is so severe. Besides, I've got this." Sugar sounded more determined than upbeat.

It hit Jackson with a pang that Lynette must be pregnant. Hank must be pleased as punch to be a father. Jackson had never really thought about having a baby. They didn't really fit in space, but he thought maybe one day he'd like to have a child. He'd have to move back to Earth for it, but that wouldn't be so bad when his days would be spent watching a son or daughter grow up.

"I know you do," Lynette said. "But my unsolicited advice would be to make sure the contestants have activities to do at all times or you'll end up with mayhem on your hands."

"I kind of don't have time to amuse them right now." Sugar's voice was mild, but she was clearly annoyed at the advice.

"They will end up amusing themselves if you don't create an activity for them. Make them play a game. Maybe a scavenger hunt? Something. But idle hands lead to full-scale drama."

Sugar sighed in defeat. "No, you're right. I'll come up with something for them to do. Talk to you guys at 1pm." She slapped disconnect button, silencing more advice. "Let's go see if we can find Russ in the speakeasy. If he's there, don't let me kill him."

CHAPTER FIVE

*E*thel's Speakeasy was located a block toward the theater, but they took the golf cart anyway. Sugar figured the way this job was going, she might need it at a moment's notice.

She was silently trying to talk herself off the ledge of annoyance she was balanced on. When Lynette had warned her that the contestants had to be entertained at all times, Sugar had known she was right. She just had enough on her plate right now without having to amuse grown adults who should be able to spend a few hours by themselves without breaking out into drama.

As much as she didn't have time, she would have to do it. The last thing she needed was to end up with a hair-pulling, ear-splitting fight.

The speakeasy turned out to be down a set of stone steps in the basement. Next to the door, a discreet sign read *Ethel's Speakeasy – Password Required.*

"Huh. That's kind of cool." Sugar had always thought secret societies seemed glamorous. Although she supposed anyone could come here if they paid to get into the park. Still, it was a cool concept. It made her think of flappers and gin gimlets. She'd always wanted to dance the Charleston and wear a feather in a headband. Past eras in history always had such amazing fashion.

"So, if you don't have a password, you can't get in?"

Jackson asked, his presence taking up way too much space as far as she was concerned.

"I guess so. This park is really amazing." She wished she had more time to explore. Maybe when filming was over and the park reopened, she'd come back as a tourist. It was probably packed as hell all the time. The last time she went to Disney, she spent the whole day standing in lines and sweating her ass off. Still, the concept was so awesome. She promised herself she'd try to find some time to explore after all this was over. She rarely took vacations, since her life was dictated by filming schedules, but maybe she'd come here in between shows instead of lying around her apartment watching reality TV. Not that she was totally goofing off, since it was research. She needed to keep up with the latest and greatest. It was, after all, her livelihood. It used to drive her boyfriend Tom crazy that she watched such bad TV, and he constantly made fun of her for it. As a doctor, Tom didn't respect her job at all. She had finally wised up that he looked down on her for what she did and she'd kicked him out. She deserved someone who respected her and her chosen profession.

Instead of being locked, which is what she expected, the doorknob turned under her hand and they went along a narrow hall for some time before they met a steel door with a small sliding cutout in the middle. She could imagine knocking once, then three times, the slider opening to reveal only a set of eyes looking at her.

Instead, no one waited for them, and this door, too, was unlocked. After the apartments needing to be opened by Niles, this easy access puzzled her. "Russ must have gotten Niles to unlock the doors for him. Maybe he's been here this whole time putting cameras everywhere."

"Yeah," Jackson agreed, staring into the dark recesses of a coat closet behind a counter, then at the small door behind a hostess stand. "It's kind of spooky when everything is empty and dark like this, isn't it?"

It was. In fact, the whole park had an odd stillness to

it, as if they were being watched.

They passed into the speakeasy itself, straight into the world of flappers and zoot suits, the atmosphere super lux, even in the dim half-light.

The space was cavernous, lit by a single spotlight on the far stage, done in black and gold, the wallpaper geometric art deco patterns. The temperature was cool, almost cold, the smell of stale alcohol and cigarette smoke still lingering, even though she'd read the park was strictly non-smoking. A long bar ran the length of the wall to the right and tables filled the rest of the area, all pristinely cleaned with an unlit candle in the center and chairs meticulously pushed in at exactly in the five and seven positions, facing the stage. As if everyone who came here would sit in groups of two.

The sight reminded her of how America was the land of the couple. Couples were the base unit for any trip, in any restaurant, and any activity. Sugar had loved being part of a couple, but in the end, she realized being alone was better than being with the wrong guy. She'd rather go eat at a nice restaurant with a girlfriend than end up wishing she'd never let an asshole move in after he stiffed her yet again on his half of the rent. Plus, she could eat cereal for dinner standing at her kitchen island rather than have someone pressuring her to make a big meal with a meat, a vegetable, and a starch. She was a firm believer that the vitamins they sprayed on cereal were almost as good as the real deal.

She spotted Russ' huge backpack with all his camera equipment on one of the tables closest to the stage. "He's here," she said, pointing, feeling a large amount of relief. "He must be in the back room routing cameras." She struck out across the room, repeating the mantra that she would not kill Russ when she found him, because she needed him for her job to be successful. Besides, she'd always liked Russ, despite the fact he made her crazy with his Russ-ness.

"Russ?" She pushed through the door marked with the ubiquitous *Employee's Only* and down a short, steep set of steps into the real basement.

Immediately the hipster flapper vibe disappeared to reveal stark concrete walls and chipped tile floors. Low lighting illuminated what appeared to be an underground tunnel that ran the length of International Street, or possibly the whole park. The tunnel was big enough to drive a small car through and she could see at least two doorways vaguely visible down the hall. It smelled damp to her and it was hotter down here.

"Russ?" she called again, her voice echoing back to her.

"Think he went down the hall?" Jackson didn't sound sure. Because why would he?

"I guess we should go make sure."

The light danced over the small plaques on each door which declared the shops above. Morty's Magical Knick Knacks, the Last Minute Quick Shop, Barney's Menagerie, but all the doors were locked, so they moved on.

She and Jackson went until the hallway ended in a T, but Russ still didn't appear. "Where is he?" she couldn't help but ask, despite knowing Jackson had no clue either.

Jackson looked first left, then right down the tunnel as he shrugged off his suit jacket, tucked it under his arm and rolled up his sleeves in the extra heat. In either direction was more of the same low lighting and periodic doorways. "You don't think he went exploring, do you?"

"Why would he? We are here to work and Russ knows that." If she was honest, she'd admit she'd been happy to be on a show with Russ again. He was a bit of a goofball, but he did his job and he did it well. Overall, she liked him, and this behavior really took her by surprise since it wasn't like him.

"Which way?"

"Go right and you'll never go wrong," Sugar said, leading the way along another tunnel, through one side of double fire doors, the bar pushing in easily beneath her hands, although part of her thought they'd gone too far. Russ would never stray this far from where he was working. "These tunnels seem to go on forever."

"I don't think he's down here," Jackson said, walking a few steps into a matching tunnel to all the other tunnels. It stretched out before them into who knew where.

"I don't either," she agreed, stepping fully on the other side of the fire door. "Russ?" she called. The door shut behind them and made a strange snapping sound as it came to rest on its soft close hinges.

They both stopped at the noise.

"Uh oh," Jackson said.

As she said, "That wasn't a good sound."

"No," he said and tried to the door.

It stayed shut, clearly locked.

"I can't believe this," she said, because she couldn't. Surely the gods didn't hate her this much?

"Me either." He rattled the door but it remained closed despite the fact he put his considerable strength into trying to open it if his bulging arms were any indication.

For a moment, she zoned out gazing at his biceps, the corded muscle and bare skin where he'd rolled up his shirt capturing her. She must be an arm luster and have never known it, because her fingers itched to touch him.

We're trapped, she reminded herself, pulling away from the fantasy.

"You've got to be kidding me." She looked around for inspiration. There was no helpful box with a hammer that said, "break glass in an emergency." What the hell were they supposed to do now? She had a show to run, contestants who were waiting for her to amuse them. A missing cameraman. Injured people. She had no time for this.

Also making her crazy was the fact she was now so turned around, she wasn't even sure where she was any more. They'd been walking far enough they could be under the amphitheater for all she knew.

Jackson rattled the door handle again, but it remained

stubbornly locked.

They were trapped.

⌣

Jackson studied the tunnel, figuring it probably ran the length of the park, not liking the situation, but not panicking either. "There has to be another exit eventually. There can't just be one place to access these halls, not with all the rooms there are down here filled with what the signs say are supplies for the shops above. That wouldn't make sense if they have to go around through the speakeasy to get them."

"Maybe there is an entrance to every store in each supply room?" Sugar guessed, shining her light on a room marked *Last Minute Quick Shop*. She tried the doorknob but while it turned in her hand, the door seemed to be barred from the other side.

"We could break into one if we have to." A bad feeling was growing in his gut, and he wasn't one to ignore his internal warning system. Where was Russ? And why hadn't they seen anyone from the park except Niles? And where had even Niles gone to after he greeted them hours ago? The whole thing didn't make sense.

They went along the hall, trying the doors of every room, which were all locked, until finally they found one marked Bob's Billiards. "I think this is located deeper into the park," Sugar said, shining her flashlight onto the sign.

"The knob is locked, so it probably isn't barred on the other side." Jackson got out his lock picks.

"What are you doing?" Sugar asked.

"I'm going to pick the lock."

"You can do that?"

"It was a childhood hobby," he said, but while the doorknob turned after he was finished, the door stayed closed, latched somehow on the other side. "We should keep going until we find a room that isn't so protected." They would have to keep trying until they found one. Eventually

51

there would be a door that wasn't barred on the inside.

"Okay." She looked behind them. "The way back is blocked by the fire door, so we'll have to keep going."

"We should stay under International Street if we can, since that will give us more opportunities to reach the surface. Once we get deeper into the park, the rides have more space between them. Assuming the tunnels even continue that far."

"Why would they have these tunnels under the whole park? The cost had to have been astronomical."

"Maybe to move supplies around while staying out of the public. I bet this place is filled with people when the park is open," he guessed. It had to be part of the experience to keep things hidden or they wouldn't have spent the money to keep everything below the surface.

They went forward, silently trying doors, but the more turns they made, the more he wasn't sure where they were any more. It was like they were in a maze.

"Wait!" Sugar said, and they both stood there looking at a sign that said Morty's Magical Knick Knacks. "How is this possible? We didn't go through a fire door to get here."

"Yeah," he said, taking the flashlight from her and shining it in a circle. "Was the door on the left or the right last time?"

"Left," she said, but not as if she was 100% sure. "It's like we're in one of those old-time haunted houses in the part where they turn you around and gaslight you."

He walked back toward where the fire doors had been in his memory.

"Don't leave me!" she said, hustling to keep up. "This is starting to creep me out."

He had no desire to leave her, but he didn't say that. Instead he swept the flashlight onto the now open fire doors. "Now they're open."

"You don't think they're on some sort of automated timer, do you?"

He studied the back of the door, but saw no

mechanism for that to happen. "Nope. Someone's jacking with us."

"But there is no one here except Barbara and Niles, and they wouldn't purposely waste our time by trapping us down here. Maybe Niles was looking for us and knew to prop the doors open? Or Russ came through here."

"Maybe." But that seemed odd to him. How would Niles even know they were down here? Possibly there were cameras he hadn't spotted because he was too distracted by Sugar. He needed to pay more attention, since this place was giving him a weird vibe. He hadn't had a feeling like this since Alphie took over the space station and tried to kill the guests.

He retraced their steps, turning left, then right, then he saw the opening that led to the short hallway and set of stairs to the speakeasy.

"The staircase," Sugar said, her voice full of relief, and hustled up the darkened steps.

Half way, her foot slipped and he caught her easily before she fell, pulling her into his chest, the smell of her shampoo filling his head with herbs and lemon. The feel of her in his arms flooded him with endorphins and a heady dollop of desire.

In the darkness, she shifted and he could tell she tipped her head up. Rather than do the prudent thing, he pressed his lips to hers, hitting her mouth perfectly, even at the awkward angle. Frisson zipped along his lips and straight down to his groin.

Instead of pulling back as he expected, she opened her mouth and slipped her tongue inside to touch his, proving the instant attraction he felt for her wasn't one sided.

Need coursed through him, punching him in the gut, feeling both wonderful and unwanted, since he was kissing the one person on the show who he wasn't supposed to kiss. He told himself to stop, but the fact was, he didn't want to.

She turned to meld her body along the length of his, her location one step up giving her just the right amount of height to make them fit together perfectly.

For a moment, they delved deep, exploring each other, her hands twisting tight into his shirt and his running up the sides of her body, following the curve of her hips to rest on her waist where he could shift them the smallest amount and he'd be cupping her breasts. He resisted the urge, even though he knew sex with Sugar would be amazing.

Then she pushed on his chest, weakly at first, then more insistent and he forced his mind to function and his hands to disengage.

In the dark, she groped around for a second before she put her hand on his shoulder. "Listen."

From the tone he knew what was coming. "I'm listening," he said, fascinated to hear if she was going to admit their natural attraction to each other, or she was going to deny it. Because if she denied it, he was calling bullshit. No one kissed like she had if they weren't into it.

But he also knew that if she said she wanted him, she would be opening herself up to risk on so many levels, especially if he chose to be an asshole about it. But since he wasn't an asshole and had no desire to lie about his feelings despite the fact liking her was a disaster of major proportions, he propped one shoulder against the wall and gave her his full attention.

"We've got something weird happening between us," she said, her voice stressed as she worked up to what he suspected was going to be the kiss-off.

"You mean our instant attraction and chemistry?" he asked, keeping his voice innocent. Because whatever this weird thing between them was, he had no doubt that sex would be off the charts.

"Well..." She seemed to struggle for a moment as she processed his honesty. "That's one way to characterize it. And while I'm sure you'd be really fun to date in the real world, we are not currently in the real world. We are on a reality TV show and in a few short weeks, you'll be leaving here engaged." She paused, then said, "To someone else."

"I see," he said. And he did. If ever there was an impossible situation, his attraction to Sugar was it. She was literally the only person in Atlantis to whom he couldn't have a relationship. Well, he supposed he couldn't date Cindy or the mysterious Barbara either. But the point was, it was a terrible idea to kiss her, but he still had. And he really wanted to again.

"It's absolutely against the rules for us to fraternize in any way," Sugar went on.

"I bet." He probably should have read the rules, but there had been so many of them and the couple pages he read had all seemed so basic and self-explanatory. Besides, he hadn't planned to break any rules because he hadn't met Sugar yet.

Okay, back up. He wasn't planning to break any rules now, either, since his next trip to space was contingent on his good behavior.

"From now on, there will be no touching of any kind between us." She sounded very sure.

He ran his fingers up her arm and pressed his palm into her hand where it still rested on his shoulder. "I see."

She shivered at the contact and snatched her hand away with a huff. "I was only touching you so I could see where you were standing," she said, defensively. "I'm trying to set boundaries here and you're laughing at me."

"Oh, I'm very much *not* laughing at you," he assured her, missing her touch already. He wondered if he could get away with kissing her again, but then figured he better not press his luck. Sugar would have to come to him. There was no other way for it to happen. "Well, then, now that you've set boundaries—"

"I have!"

"We should rejoin the show."

"Right," she said, flummoxed by his easy acquiescence. He could tell Sugar was not a woman who would do a single thing she didn't think was her idea.

So, he'd wait her out. He had until he left for space to convince her.

That's a horrible idea.

Yeah, it is, he agreed. He should pick one of the other women, but he had a bad feeling he wasn't going to listen to his own wisdom.

He followed her as she stomped up the stairs, wondering, based on her comment about the other women in the contest, if she was one of those who wouldn't live in space. He could see her adding a lot to a space station. Her organizational skills alone were worth their weight in gold.

Reality hit him then. He was supposed to be courting other women. The thought brought his raging desire to a stuttering halt. He had given his word he'd take the dating process seriously when he'd signed the contract with Hank. Which meant he had to put Sugar aside, chemistry or no chemistry. Sugar drawing boundaries was a good thing for them both. He just wished he didn't want her so badly.

How the hell had he ended up in this mess?

CHAPTER SIX

Sugar knew she was being irrational, but did he have to agree so readily to her ground rules? He could have at least put up a small fight, just a tiny protest that he liked her.

Although he'd been the one to call what was between them chemistry. A loaded word if ever she heard one.

What was she doing? This job was her big break. She wasn't going to screw it up by flirting with and kissing and ogling the talent. Lynette had once warned her that some women who worked on these shows found out that it was the men who were absolutely off limits who were an aphrodisiac. If it turned out that Sugar was one of those women, she needed to work on a different type of reality TV show. As long as she didn't ruin this chance, there was no shame in having to pivot away from dating and working with hoarders or addicts, which were much easier to resist on every level.

Sugar had always thought those women must have been idiots, but maybe she shouldn't have been so quick to judge. Just because she'd worked three previous seasons on The Bachelor and never once had her heart flutter didn't mean she wasn't susceptible. Obviously.

All thoughts of Jackson vanished (thank God) when she rounded the corner from the stairwell and found Russ up on a small ladder working on the stage.

"Where the hell have you been?" she asked, unable to stop herself from sounding angry because a small piece of her had been worried for him. A large piece of her was pissed he'd wandered away when she needed him.

"You're not going to believe this," he said, not bothering to look away from whatever he was screwing into the ceiling.

"This better be good," she warned, fully prepared to take her current frustrations out on the cameraman. Who was her friend, she reminded herself. *You don't kill your friends.* That was another rule she felt like breaking.

"I fell through the trap door on the stage." He pointed to the center of the stage floor with his screwdriver.

"What?" She and Jackson came onto the stage like neighbors to a house fire.

"Careful," Russ warned. "It has a hair trigger. It took me forever to get out of there, too. I was trapped in some sort of weird circle down in the tunnels below us."

Jackson put the tip of his toe on the trapdoor, which immediately began to collapse under the slight weight "What is this place? It's like a fun house that isn't fun at all."

"I'm bruised as hell too." Russ climbed down from the ladder. He arched backwards and winced. "I think I pulled something in my back."

"We went to look for you and were stuck in a circle, too." She wondered what her next step was going to be, because she couldn't have contestants running around the park falling through floors and disappearing. How the hell was she supposed to work under these conditions? She was only one woman. Resisting the urge to rage, she focused on the practical. She'd have to rope off the stage when they had the first mixer so no one got it into their heads to start dancing and ended up one story below with a concussion.

She should change the venue, but there wasn't time to find another place to host it and the rest of the speakeasy was the perfect back drop. She'd have to emphasize that no one was allowed to explore and warn them all of the consequences. *Like that would work.* Keeping contestants contained was like herding cats. At least one woman would end up in the tunnels even with the caution. It was in some people's nature to do things they were told not to.

You should know all about that.

This could be a new type of reality TV, one where the last woman standing got the guy. Kind of horror meets dating show. She could pitch it to Hank and see if he had any interest. The way things were going, they were filming that show right now.

"I need to talk to Hank again, but first we should move Cindy. She's probably wondering if we have abandoned her." Because they had abandoned her. Which was terrible. She should have moved Cindy, then looked for Russ. But how was she supposed to know she'd end up trapped in the tunnels? Especially since she hadn't even known there were tunnels.

"It's past 1pm," Jackson said, staring at his watch.

"Oh crap," she said. They'd been in the tunnels longer than she'd realized. "We move Cindy first, even if that means we miss talking to Hank."

She and Jackson left the speakeasy at a light jog. Sugar figured by the end of filming, she'd finally be in shape. She always meant to be, but never quite got there. She blamed her best friend Merlot. Her least favorite part of being on set was the strict rule of no alcohol for the staff. She would give up a body part for a glass of red right now.

Zipping to the theater, she found Cindy still sitting against the wall. "Oh God, I'm so glad you're here. I need to pee so badly."

Poor Cindy. "Let us help you get there." Hank would just have to suck up their lateness.

"I can pick you up while Sugar keeps your leg still." Jackson waited until Sugar nodded agreement, then gently picked Cindy up, while Sugar kept her foot supported.

"Oh, it hurts," Cindy said, as they went sideways through the bathroom door. Finally, they had her seated on the commode after much jostling. They stood outside the stall door while she moaned in relief. "That was so close."

Jackson grimaced at Sugar in sympathy and she frowned in agreement.

After the kiss on the stairs, she needed to firmly entrench Jackson in his room, but she had to admit, his help with Cindy was invaluable. Her next priority should be physically separating herself from Jackson so her libido could calm down. After they had Cindy in her room, that would be job number one.

They had to reverse the process to get Cindy out of the bathroom and all the way out into the golf cart. She was in obvious pain when Jackson finally carried her into her room and deposited her gently on the bed, propping her leg with pillows.

"Let me grab you some ice to put on that knee," Sugar said, finally remembering some basic first aid skills. She went into the kitchen and dumped every bit of ice from the freezer in a plastic bag, then grabbed dish towels and returned.

"I'll come back and help you into the bathroom in a couple hours," Jackson was promising as she came in and helped Cindy arrange the ice and towels.

Jackson Wright was a very nice guy. He didn't have to be so kind to Cindy, but he had been. And without the cameras rolling, too. It was this fact that had Sugar shelving her idea to banish him to his room until they were ready for filming.

They returned to the magic shop, with Sugar reflecting that somehow, Jackson had become her right-hand man. She knew she needed to put some space between them. Not later, but now. "Why don't you go check on Russ at the speakeasy? I'll let you know what Hank says." After she spoke with Hank, she needed to come up with an activity of some sort for the contestants to do. "Tell Russ he needs to be ready to film the contestants in an hour during their activity."

He hesitated and she thought he might refuse.

Instead, he said, "Sure, Sugar," and left without argument.

Suddenly, Sugar had a bad feeling she'd done the wrong thing. She should have kept Jackson with her instead of going it alone like she always did. Something about Atlantis made her reconsider her belief that she was better off relying only on herself. There were other people who could be trusted to do what they promised to do and she was pretty sure Jackson was one of them.

She pushed the unwelcome thought aside and went to talk to Hank. Their rescue had better be on the way. She wasn't sure she could keep things running on her own for two more days.

⸺

Jackson found Russ leaving the speakeasy.

"Hey man," Russ said, hefting a large backpack on his back. "You any good with electronics?"

"Actually, I am," Jackson said, figuring that helping Russ would be better than being locked in his room for hours with nothing to do. The pack list had specifically forbidden reading material. He supposed he could draw out specs for his cardio-in-space project, but he had a bad feeling he'd spend the time obsessing about whatever it was that was happening between him and Sugar.

It turned out Russ was going to Jackson's room anyway. He spread out his tools and electronics and had Jackson pass everything to him without much discussion.

After, they moved on to the common area and started setting up a camera there.

"Are we going to have any filming events here?" Jackson asked, wondering why they were putting cameras here and in the hallway.

"I have to pick up any of your movements to make sure you're covered." Russ screwed in the mount for the camera to the ceiling.

"Why?" If he looked at filming the Bachelor objectively, really the mechanics of the show were fascinating.

"You'd be surprised how many bachelors try to sneak around and meet up with the contestants outside of normal filming hours. Happens at least every other show."

"Seriously?" Didn't they get enough of the contestants during filming?

"Yeah. On Mars, Chad Harper slipped off into a storage closet to have sex hours after we arrived, beating out the Bachelor from two seasons before who took 48 hours to accomplish unsanctioned nookie. Now we film the Bachelor's room, hallway and any areas he has access to."

"Great." Jackson shook his head, not liking the fact he would have to lock himself in his rather small bathroom to get away from the cameras. *You signed up for this*, he reminded himself. He had. He didn't have any right to feel sorry for himself, but he still did.

"You're pretty good at this," Russ said. "Want to install the one in the hall while I finish up here?"

"Sure." Jackson loved working with his hands, especially on technical things. It kept his mind busy and away from unwanted thoughts, like the fact he should never have agreed to become the Bachelor.

After they'd finished wiring this side of the street, Russ said, "Listen, I've got to follow around the contestants on their activity. You okay with starting the camera installs across the street after they leave? As fast as you are, you might even complete them."

"You got it," Jackson said, willing to do anything to keep boredom and thoughts of Sugar at bay.

Sugar left the pow-wow with Hank and Lynette with a mapped-out activity for the cast. Within minutes, she'd organized the cast into two teams. Jillian and Raven on one team, which she figured evened out since Raven was still complaining of a headache and Jillian was the only cast member who hadn't been hurt. And Lena and Andi on the other, since they were both only mildly walking wounded. "This is a scavenger hunt, but instead of items, you'll be bringing back pictures." She handed them each team a sheet of paper and a cell phone. "The cell phones don't have the ability to call or text, and I've left them locked so you only have access to the cameras." The cellphones had belonged to her and Russ, although Russ had only given his up after much protest. She would have had the teams bring back items, but since the doors were supposed to be locked except in specific places according to their contract, she instead sent them to take selfies in front of the rides and various attractions she'd picked at random from her map in the farthest locations she could find. This game was designed to keep them busy and out of her hair.

"Bob's Billiards?" Raven asked, reading the first entry off their sheet. "Willie's Ragtime Theater? Who named these places? It's like we time warped back into the past."

"It's part of the park's theme." Personally, Sugar adored the 1920's and wished she'd fully appreciated the flapper vibe before she'd arrived so she could have had the costumers come up with 1920's outfits for the first night's mixer. She wondered what Jackson would look like in a zoot suit, then squashed the idea. One of Sugar's secret joys was dressing up for Halloween. There was nothing better than a holiday devoted to costumes, candy, and alcohol. "Here is the challenge. You need to take selfies of yourselves at each of these locations with the cellphones. The fastest team gets an advantage that will be announced at the appropriate time. You will be glad you have it, I promise you." Sugar had no idea what the advantage would be. She'd have to figure it out later, because right now she couldn't come up with a single idea.

All four women had gotten dressed up for the activity, but Sugar had made them change into tennis shoes, assuring them no one would ever know that they weren't wearing heels.

"Make sure the pictures are good, because they will be used if they are, online *and* in social media promos."

That had everyone but Jillian smiling. Jillian had been decidedly quiet and her face showed clear skepticism, but Sugar knew Jillian was here for the long game so she'd play along.

Raven fluffed her hair in preparation. Sugar knew only people who liked the camera ever made it on The Bachelor. If you didn't, this would be a torturous hell. Personally, she hated having her picture taken. She always ended up with her mouth half open or her body turned in such a way it made her look the size of a house.

"Also take these, since it's getting dark. You can take pictures of each other if you need to, just make sure each of you is in front of the locations or it won't count." She passed out four flashlights, figuring it was getting dark and they would need all the light they could get.

"Your whole team has to stick together at all times. *No* cheating. Remember, we have cameras everywhere." They didn't, but thank god the contestants didn't know that, she thought as she waved goodbye to them, wishing Hank hadn't told the management to cut the cell service off. He had been thinking of the game, not possible safety concerns, but now she badly wished her cellphone worked.

If she had a working cell right now, she would call Hank every hour and ream him out for not getting help here sooner.

But Hank had been way too excited by the prospect that the contestants literally weren't able to cheat and therefore the staff's constant attentiveness could be relaxed. Four seasons ago, they'd had a woman call a tabloid to give them the scoop on the game from a gardener's phone she borrowed. Since then, Hank had been down right fanatical about letting anyone have access to the outside world.

It didn't matter that Sugar had personally searched

through every single item in the cast's suitcases, culling out a variety of banned items such as food, books, and strangely, a naked men magazine, which was a first. She could personally guarantee no one had slipped in any recording devices or cameras. Sugar had checked their luggage twice, since she almost always found *something*. Of course, she had found banned items, but they were more along the lines of fighting boredom than a flagrant flouting of the rules.

Down the street, Jillian turned back to stare at her, probably cursing Sugar under her breath when she realized what a slog this was going to be.

Sugar waved at her and she could almost see Jillian rolling her eyes as she hurried to catch Raven, who had left her standing there. Rule number one of the scavenger hunt was that they had to stick together as a team.

Sugar went back up to the apartment lounge to get her own luggage from the stack. She'd sweated through her deodorant and needed to freshen up a bit. Maybe brush her hair. And she had to pee. After taking care of that first, she stared at her reflection in the mirror, aghast at what she saw. She looked like she'd been mowed down by a Mack truck.

Sadly, there wasn't time for a shower, which was probably the only way she could un-limp-ify her hair, so she had to settle for brushing it out and redoing her ponytail. Then deodorant and some lip gloss.

You better not be dolling yourself up on purpose, she told herself, because she knew there was only one person who would remotely care about her limp hair. And it wasn't Russ.

You will not lust after the Bachelor. Period. Dot. She stared at her reflection, frowning with her newly hydrated lips, resisting the urge to add some eye makeup. These were the actions of a woman who liked a man. A man who was totally off limits to her. A man who she not only should not like, but who was totally unsuited for her.

Taking the show completely out of the equation, which was silly because her job was everything to her, Jackson

Wright wanted to live his foreseeable life on a space station. Which was at best impractical for dating life and at worst wackadoodle. Yes, on the surface it was a super cool career, but really, who wanted a man with a life goal of being a gazillion miles away for months or years at a time?

Not her, no matter how charming his dimple.

Even if she was willing to put her job aside, which she wasn't, they weren't destined to be together long term and Sugar was tired of short term. So tired, she had made an unbreakable agreement with herself not to ever go for *light and fun* again.

Ergo, she would delete the earlier kiss from her memory bank.

That decided, she threw the eyeliner unused in her bag, only to see something move out the bathroom window.

Niles sat on a bench in the fake grassy park below, looking through the bubble into the lake at the fish swimming by. Or possibly he was meditating, since he was sitting completely still. He could be a statue except she'd recognize that black getup he was wearing anywhere.

She had no idea where he'd been, but she needed some answers and she needed them now. Atlantis had promised them a support crew and so far, they'd had exactly ten minutes of Niles' 'support' and nothing from Barbara, who had been completely MIA.

It was time to put her inappropriate attraction to the talent aside and do her job.

Hoofing it double time out the front, since that was the only direction she could go, she raced down the street, turned left twice, and raced back the other direction before Niles could disappear again. She didn't slow until she saw him still sitting on the bench.

She really had expected him to be gone by the time she made it down the long block, so she hadn't prepared what she was going to say when she arrived. "Niles," she said, using her best Head Wrangler voice around the gasping she was doing, since she had beat feet to get here.

Niles didn't turn to acknowledge her presence.

A creeping feeling rode over her... What if he'd been so still because he was dead?

"Oh my God," she whispered, and grabbed his shoulder as she rounded the bench.

He jumped then, and flinched away from her, giving her a startled and unfriendly look.

"Oh, I'm sorry," she said, not adding that she'd thought he was dead, as that seemed a bit silly, since he wasn't.

"Did you need something?" Niles narrowed his eyes in clear annoyance.

She straightened, pushing aside her embarrassment for manhandling him. "I did, yes. Our contract with Atlantis said you owe us assistance in setting up the rides and other needs. Yet we have barely had any support from the Atlantis staff since we arrived."

He gave her a long stare, filled with absolutely no emotion at all. As if to say *I don't care about you or the contract.*

Sugar found him super disconcerting and resisted the urge to turn and walk away. Her job was to make Niles and his fellow Atlantis workers do their jobs. That was the cornerstone of a Wrangler's responsibilities. "How about I take my complaints to Barbara? Where is she, by the way?"

"There he is!" Niles stood and pointed, his face changing completely, excitement in every grim line.

She turned to see a large, grayish silver fish swimming toward them. "Oh," she said, not sure what to say, because it was a really big fish. It could qualify as gigantic, longer than her arm.

Growing up, her father had taken her fishing, but she had only caught small minnows and hand sized sunfish. She'd found the whole thing depressing. Killing fish for a dinner she didn't even particularly like made her feel guilty. Further, she was a woman of action. Being still for hours drove her crazy. She spent the whole time sitting there thinking about everything she'd accomplish if she could just go home.

"Salvelinus namaycush," Niles said.

"What?"

"A fine specimen of lake trout." Niles put his hand on the thick plastic of the bubble and the fish swam toward him. "They can get up to one hundred pounds and he has to be close to that." Love filled the older man's face, softening it, his lips falling open on a harsh intake of breath.

Or at least she thought it was love. Whatever it was, it made his eyes sparkle and made her want to run far, far away.

"Uh, yeah," Sugar said. "So, where is Barbara exactly?" She needed to stop dealing with Niles. He was obviously a few cards short of a deck.

For a moment, the fish mouthed where Niles' hand pressed to the bubble. Niles made a sound that was half hum, half *awwww*.

Then the fish startled and zipped away.

"Dammit," Niles said, pointing ten feet to the left at something else shiny and silver that was in no way a fish.

"What is that?" She approached the bubble, not sure what she was looking at. It was some sort of robot on the other side, about four feet long and a foot wide, slowly moving along the plastic.

"It's supposed to clean the algae off the bubble, but it's a fish killer," Niles said, spitting in his fury. He pounded on the bubble as if trying to dislodge it, but the robot simply zoomed along, oblivious.

Okayyyyy. Niles was nuts. That settled it. She needed to work with someone else. "Barbara." She kept her voice as firm as she could. "Where is she right now?" She had so much to do, but she would stop everything to find her Atlantis contact and convince her that Niles would not be the best liaison between them due to the fact he was clearly insane.

"They sweep along and if the fish don't see them, they will chew the fish into pieces. Harold has been around too long to get caught, but the younger ones do at a steady clip.

The park thinks that restocking the lake makes up for their wonton destruction, but it doesn't."

"Who is Harold?" Had Atlantis provided another worker? Perhaps Harold could help instead.

"The Salvelinus namaycush!" Spittle flew with his vehemence.

"Uh huh. That is a bummer," she said, backing away. And it was, but she didn't have time to save the world. She had a show to wrangle.

Niles banged on the bubbled again, cursing at the cleaning robot. "Get away from here. Go!"

While his back was turned, she escaped.

She needed to call Hank and get an update. Maybe he would know where she could find Barbara, because she was done with Niles. She wasn't paid enough to deal with crazy. Well, except for crazy contestants. There were always one or two of those.

Double timing it, she reached Morty's and through the front door just in time to hear the phone ringing. She slapped the phone on speaker. "Sugar," she said.

"It's Hank."

"Good. I was just coming in to call you." Sugar dragged the hair tie from her hair, shook it out, then put the ponytail back up again since it had half fallen during her escape.

"We have a firm ETA for you, but you're not going to like it."

Of course she wasn't. Because God hated her. That had to be it. "Just say it Hank." She really wasn't in the mood for drawn out Hankisms where he tried to convince her it wasn't as bad as it sounded.

"We can be down there in forty-eight hours," he said, as if she couldn't do the math and discover that was two whole days.

"Cindy is going to be in agony," she warned, but she knew it was futile to complain. Although she still wanted to.

The fact was, Hank would be down here as fast as he could. Not to rescue her, but because time was burning and the longer he delayed, the harder it was going to be to condense filming. As it was, they would need to run the last two episodes somewhere else. The Bachelor sleeping with three women couldn't be crunched down past three nights. Hank had tried that already and it had been a huge disaster.

She veered away sharply from thinking about Jackson sleeping with three different women. "You need to figure out where the nurse's station is so I can get some more painkillers." She hadn't seen it on her map

"I can do that," he said, sounding relieved she hadn't flipped out on him, although what good would it do to flip out, really?

She was paid to keep things running against all odds and that's what she would do. "Also, I need you to find out where Barbara is."

"She's not with you?"

"I haven't seen her."

"Have you checked the Administration Building?"

"No," she said between clinched teeth. "Because I did not know there *was* an Administration Building."

"Down by the Catering Pavilion. I would start there. I'll ask around on my end and see if I can get a landline number for her, since they have an old-time phone system there. Did you find Russ?" he asked, as if he suddenly remembered.

"Yeah. He ended up falling through a trapdoor on the stage where our first cocktail will take place."

"What?"

"Never mind." She needed Hank to focus on her current problems. Russ had returned. At this point, she had bigger worries. "I need Barbara. Niles is completely crazy."

"Who is Niles?"

"Some guy who works for Atlantis."

The sound of flipping paper came over the speaker. "I don't have anyone named Niles on the list. It's supposed to be Barbara and John."

"Maybe they had to replace him with Niles?" Not that she cared. She needed Hank to focus. "I'll go straight over to the Admin Building. I can't deal with Niles. He's nutty as a bedbug." She needed to ask Hank for everything she wanted now, while he felt guilty. "I need Lynette to brainstorm some more things I can do with the cast that are down here. I sent them off on a scavenger hunt a few minutes ago with Russ to film them." She might as well have Lynette use her brain, while Sugar ran around putting out fires.

"I'll get her working on a list for the next call."

"Plus, I need your permission to have a group date in the meantime to burn some hours."

"No," Hank said before she'd finished talking.

"Hank," she said, raising her voice. "There is one of me and five of them. I cannot keep them occupied on my own. You and I both know boredom is a recipe for disaster."

Hank sighed. "Let me think about it."

"It's three o'clock right now," she said, glancing at her watch to see it was really three-thirty. "I need an answer by tomorrow morning. I want to have the group date at lunch. I'll dress them up as if it's dinner and they can do something like a photoshoot with the Bachelor or maybe I'll spray them down with water and have them mud wrestle." Although the thought of Jackson rolling around in mud with other women grossed her out.

Suddenly she didn't want to do this job any more. She wanted to quit instead of watch Jackson date other women for the next month.

No, she was a *Professional*. With a capital P. She was going to personally spray Jackson down herself and throw a bikini clad contestant at him. Four of them, actually. Because she wasn't going to freak out and quit her job.

Because she was a PROFESSIONAL. Dammit.

"Let me talk to Lynette before you ruin things by putting them together. The first night is supposed to be where the Bachelor instinctively gets rid of the women he doesn't have chemistry with. If he knows some of them already, he'll feel pressure to treat them differently."

She knew what the first date was for. "I want ideas by tomorrow morning. I need to find Barbara and get some things rolling with the Atlantis staff." And check on the contestants to make sure nothing had gone wrong. It would be bad if one of them had fallen through a trap door.

"Let's talk at nine tomorrow then."

"Great," she said, enjoying hanging up on him before he could say goodbye, suddenly antsy.

She left Morty's with a bad feeling something was going wrong somewhere in the park.

CHAPTER SEVEN

*J*ackson crossed the street to start setting up the contestants' camera feeds. He veered to pick up a water from the back of one of the carts, cracking the seal as he considered what a cluster this whole thing had turned out to be.

Taking a long swig, he watched Sugar come out of Morty's Magical Knick Knacks and stride toward him. She looked pissed. And beautiful. He sighed.

"Why are you in the street?" she asked snappishly.

"Whoa," he said and held up both hands, the water bottle dangling from one of them. "I'm helping Russ with the wiring in the women's apartments."

She relented almost immediately. "Okay." She shook her head. "I'm sorry. I'm just royally annoyed at Hank and I was taking it out on you. Of course you know how to wire things. I should have realized that Russ is just as short-handed as I am and pressing you into service makes sense."

"It's really better than sitting alone and bored in my room."

"I bet."

"When is our rescue inbound?" he asked, hating to put more pressure on her, but really wanting to know. When Hank arrived, Jackson knew it was the beginning of the end of his freedom.

"Forty-eight hours." She blew out a breath and rubbed her eyes with a hand. "I know, I know. I felt the same," she replied to whatever he emotion he had on his face.

He hadn't even said anything. There was no reason to bitch. It wasn't like it was her fault they were stuck down here. Giving Sugar a hard time would just add to her stress and accomplish nothing. "What can I do to help?"

"Have you checked on Cindy?"

"Yeah, she's good." The swelling on her knee had gone down significantly with ice and anti-inflammatories but putting any weight on it was obviously very painful, even though she tried to stay positive.

"I have to go to the Administration Building." She consulted her clipboard, which was with her as always. "It's down by the Catering Pavilion."

His stomach rumbled at the thought of food. "So about food…" he trailed off and gave her a hopeful look.

She sighed. "Food. I'd totally forgotten food. There are MREs down at the Catering Pavilion. Why don't you take the other cart and bring a few crates back? Put a couple in the contestants' apartments and at least one in our side." She jumped in the first golf cart.

He climbed into the other, more than ready to abandon his work for Russ if it meant food. He followed her down to the warehouse. He'd been hungry for hours but hadn't wanted to add to her burdens.

Sugar didn't get out at the Pavilion. "I have to go find Barbara from the Atlantis staff in the Admin Building, then I'm going to go try to catch up with the contestants and bring them water."

"Have they eaten?"

She frowned. "I bet not."

Have you eaten? he wanted to ask, but didn't. Sugar could take care of herself. "Do you want to at least take them a snack?"

"I'll bring them something to tide them over." Unhappily, she dismounted and joined him in the warehouse and fished out a big box marked *snacks*.

He carried out another case of water and placed it on the back of her cart while she put the snacks beside her on the bench seat.

"See you later," he said, feeling oddly like his wife was leaving for work.

She gave him a strange look and drove down to park outside the building that looked like a fake Southern mansion.

He watched her march up the short set of stairs and try the door. It opened and she walked inside. He had an odd desire to wait for her.

For the first time in his adult life, Jackson realized he wanted a relationship. He wanted that feeling of being attached to another person. How nice would it be to kiss someone goodbye when they left you and kiss someone hello again when they returned?

Although living in space, there would be no kissing because there would be no leaving. No one went anywhere. It was life in a small space that would be hell if he took the wrong person with him. He'd liked the solitude when he'd lived in Genesis III. He'd always been someone who could easily amuse himself. He enjoyed his own company. It was easy and he had a lot of things to do, like learning how small engines operated, or reading about the history of Mars exploration, or playing one of the million games he had saved onto his handheld. If he was ever lonely, which almost never happened, he would go find Milton and listen to stories about Milton's old ventures—the circus, the skydiving business, the upscale all-inclusive resort island. Milton had a never-ending string of experiences that never failed to amuse. Of course, he should have known Genesis III was in trouble when Milton had confessed everything he'd ever done had ended in bankruptcy. But for a long time, Jackson had been happily oblivious.

He went through the remaining crates he hadn't explored earlier, taking an inventory of the items available to him. If they were going to be stuck down here for this long without the others, he figured he could use some of the supplies. He stacked six boxes of food and more water on his cart, drove it to the apartments and distributed it all, before returning to work on the cameras again.

⌒

"Barbara," Sugar called as she walked into the Admin Building, flipping on a light beside the door. Hank was going to hyperventilate when he got the electricity bill, but Sugar was sick of being in the dark. Her flashlight was going to stay on her hip for this little adventure.

A large receptionist's desk in dark wood blocked the back of the room from outsiders. Sugar zigged around it. "Barbara?" A long hallway stretched before her and Sugar flicked on the light.

From the back of the building, someone returned her call, the word garbled.

Finally, a live body. She'd begun to think Barbara had abandoned them. Sugar wasn't going to freak out on Barbara, even though she wanted to. That would get her nowhere. She needed support and honey really did attract more flies than vinegar.

Moving along the hall, she passed offices, each with names on the closed doors. The voice had come from deep within the building, so back she went. "Barbara?" she called again. She found the stairwell with stairs heading up as well as down. She'd climbed half way up, figuring down went into the tunnels, when she heard another "Muhhh" from Barbara behind her.

Really, what was going on here? Sugar needed proactive help, not all this crazy roaming around. She stomped down the stairs, gearing up to let Barbara have a little of her frustration. Atlantis had promised two staff members. Niles did not count. Niles was a wacko. Although the contract probably didn't specify the mental state of the workers, it did state that they had to be available to the Bachelor crew.

She paused at the bottom of the steps, not completely sure which way to go. "Barbara?"

"Here," said a voice, this time more clearly, from the second office on the left.

She pushed open the door to find the room empty of furniture, with just a rug covering the center of the floor. She flipped on the light to see more clearly, sure Barbara's voice had come from here. A door was open at the other end of the room. She crossed without thinking, speeding up now that she had Barbara in her sights.

The feeling of weightlessness hit her, the floor dropping and her sudden decent taking her off guard, her stomach going *whoop!* as she plummeted downwards, the rug swathing her in an unwanted shroud, restricting her arms as they tried to pinwheel.

Quickly, she hit ground with a metal *twang*, then continued to slide downward until she rolled to a stop, the rug wrapping her like a burrito.

A loud snap sounded above her.

Panic zigged through her as she fought her way free, only to realize she was in complete darkness. She struggled to sit, dazed and confused, trying to make sense out of what just happened. Taking stock, she realized she wasn't hurt, even though she figured she really should be after all that.

Another trap door had swallowed her. It could be the only explanation. The snapping sound was most likely the door closing again on some sort of hinge. Frustration ripped through her and she had a moment when she wanted to scream. Crap. She did *not* have time for this. The contestants were even now wandering around, starving and grumpy, wondering where she was. The show was going to crater and burn without her up there managing things. Or at the very least, implode in drama.

She took a deep breath, trying for perspective, breathing through the panic. She had at least another hour or two before things went sideways. She'd sent them all over hell and back through the park.

It was several long, agonizing moments in the dark before she remembered her flashlight, still in her back pants pocket. She took it out and shined it along what appeared to be a large, metal slide that had deposited her safely at the bottom onto what seemed to be a new mattress. That solved the mystery of why she hadn't been hurt and why she couldn't feel the flashlight in her back pocket despite the fact she'd been sitting on it.

She ran the light around the room, studying the gray rock walls unbroken on all four sides. Unlike when Russ fell through at the speakeasy into the tunnels, she was in a closed room with nothing in it but the slide, a mattress, and the rug.

Someone had been calling to her before she'd fell through. She stood and focused her light at the top of the slide where she could just barely see the edges of the trapdoor.

"Barbara?" she yelled. She *had* heard someone. That's why she'd gone in the room in the first place. "Barbara!" she yelled up to the ceiling. "I fell through a trapdoor. Come help me out!"

She stopped yelling and listened.

Nothing. No sound of anyone walking around. No movement across the floors. No return yell to reassure her.

Panic touched her again when she realized that it would be at least another two days before Hank would arrive to find her. The contestants and Russ didn't even know she was down here.

Wait. Jackson knew she was here. He'd been across the street at the Pavilion picking up food for everyone when she'd entered the building. If she failed to come back, he would look for her.

She clung to that, because as weird as it sounded, she trusted him so much more than she probably should after knowing him for only a day. He would notice her absence and do something about it. He *would* come looking. Her golf cart was still outside the Admin Building, so he'd know she was here.

That didn't mean she was going to give up, though, and just sit here waiting.

She studied the slide. It was built out of a single sheet of metal that had been bent up on the sides to form a kind of trough that had slid her safely to the floor.

"What the hell is up with this place? It's insane." When she conquered the slide, she'd vote for them to leave and film someplace else. Money be damned, this location was going to get someone killed.

Holding the flashlight in her teeth, she started up the slide and immediately ended up back on the ground, her boots too slick to find purchase on the metal surface. She took off her boots and socks, wishing she wasn't barefoot but there really wasn't any other option.

She tried again, this time making it a few feet up before she dropped with a clang to her knees and slid down until she was dumped on her ass. And again, making it half way before she ended up hanging as she gripped the left side with both hands while her feet scrambled on the smooth metal, unable to steady themselves.

The slide was six feet wide, but maybe she could do some sort of Spiderman thing where she walked up the sides where the metal was a little rougher. She made it about a foot before she realized it was too wide for her to go further without popping her femur out of her hip socket. However, she couldn't seem to bring herself to let go of the sides and slide back down.

Annoyingly, she was stuck.

In frustration, she screamed, "Ahhhhhhh!" knowing it was an unhelpful waste of time but unable to stop herself from venting her massive frustration.

⌇

Russ had told Jackson to make sure to be gone by five at the latest, so Jackson packed up about fifteen till and hoofed it out of the women's apartments, having secured the cameras in all but the last two apartments which didn't currently have anyone in them.

As he'd been working, he thought about the short-wave radios he'd seen in a crate down in the warehouse. It would be better if they all had radios, especially Cindy, who could radio him if she needed anything, instead of him constantly stopping what he was doing to run across and ask her if she was okay.

He debated for a moment if Sugar would be pissed he had them. She'd been pretty clear that she didn't want him wandering around out of his room. Then he figured it would be better to beg for forgiveness than to ask permission and deviated from his path to his apartment. He climbed into the golf cart he was starting to think of as his own to go down the warehouse, hoping to be back up the street before she even noticed he was gone.

Sugar's golf cart hadn't returned, but he figured she was out and about distributing water and snacks to the contestants.

He was so focused on getting the radios as he hustled into the Catering Pavilion, he almost missed the fact Sugar's golf cart was still in front of the Admin Building where she had parked earlier. Weird. She must still be talking to the mysterious Barbara.

He found the radios where he remembered and got out two, then paused, studying the rest. Maybe everyone should carry one in case they ended up lost again or whatever. Jackson was very focused on safety first. Unable to control his love of all things technology, he grabbed the whole box and stashed them in the golf cart and climbed in.

For a moment, he stared at Sugar's cart, realizing she should have been gone by now checking on the scavenger hunt. How long did it take to talk to this Barbara person anyway? How much could they really talk about?

Barbara, you are contractually obligated to assist us.

You're right. I'll be right there.

Bam, done. But instead, it had been hours.

He started the cart, swooping in a wide turn to return to the apartments as he pulled away.

Then he kept going in a circle until he was facing the Admin Building again, not liking that she was still there.

Sugar wouldn't want him following her, but he found it was impossible to leave without knowing if she was okay. Maybe she'd fallen and couldn't get back up.

Yeah right. Like they were in a horror movie or something.

Most likely, she had already gone to check on the contestants and had come back for some reason.

He parked his cart beside hers, noting that the snacks box still sat unopened on the passenger seat. That was bad. It meant she hadn't gone to check on the other cast members, as she'd said she would. It was six o'clock now. What could she possibly need to talk to Barbara about for two hours?

Maybe they'd called Hank for an impromptu meeting or something. He'd step inside quietly and see if he could hear them. If he could and things sounded okay, he'd silently leave. That seemed reasonable.

Climbing the steps, he paused to glance up and down the street, the feeling of someone watching him riding his shoulders.

Okay, now he was just being ridiculous. There were only a handful of people even down here and most of them were far away on the scavenger hunt.

He tried the door. The handle turned and opened on well-oiled hinges. He stepped inside and listened, but the building was totally silent. The space felt empty, but Sugar wasn't going to leave her golf cart behind and walk back.

There had to be a simple explanation. Maybe the cart hadn't started, but then why would she leave without the box of snacks? It hadn't been heavy. Also, the lights in the building had been left on. If Sugar had left, she would have turned them off to save Hank's precious utility bill.

He ghosted through the front room, past what was obviously a receptionist's desk and down the hall, checking each empty office as he went by opening the doors and taking a quick peek. All empty offices had desks and chairs except one that was completely empty.

Then he arrived at the stairs. He could go up or down.

I should shout for her. But there was something in the air that had his spidey senses screaming *danger.* Like that time on Genesis III when the air handler wasn't working properly and the oxygen level had been dropping without setting off an alarm. If he hadn't gotten a "feeling," he and Milton would have most likely died.

So, he'd follow his gut on this one and stealth-look for Sugar, even if it turned out he was letting paranoia rule him. Besides, what else was he going to do? Sit in his room and twiddle his thumbs?

Mentally tossing a coin, he went upstairs. Empty. Just more offices with nameplates on the doors, filing cabinets and desks and the usual office crap. God, he'd die in a desk job like this, doing the same things day after day. He needed a job with adventure, something that threw surprises at him at every turn. A job that made his mind stay frosty.

He came back downstairs and kept going to the basement. A steel door stood at the bottom, matching the one from the speakeasy. Odd. There was no reason to have metal here when every other door was cheap plasterboard.

The hairs on his arms stood up with awareness as he noticed the big padlock hanging above the door handle. One of the old timey ones that needed a key to open. Maybe it was a supply room? Where they kept money from the daily receipts? Just in case, he ran his hand along the top of the doorway, but found only dust.

Surely Sugar wasn't trapped in what was obviously

some sort of storage room? He was letting the weirdness of a closed amusement park creep him out. But if she had somehow ended up in there, he would feel really awful if he hadn't checked.

Why would she be here? Maybe she'd gone to another building and had simply left her cart behind.

No, it made no sense for her to be trapped in the basement.

He turned and climbed back up the steps.

Without another option, he decided to go find Russ and ask him if he'd seen Sugar.

CHAPTER EIGHT

Sugar knew that screaming every time she slid to the bottom of the slide wasn't helpful, but that didn't stop her from doing it. She'd tried to climb the slide now over and over for several hours. Technique had been improved and she'd had better success, but there was one shiny spot that was extra slick that turned into her nemesis, sending her sliding backwards every time. Her whole body howled in protest at the continued abuse. Spin class twice a week hadn't prepared her for this.

She tried to convince herself that this time would be different, as she reached the highest point yet.

Just. One. More. Handhold.

She dug her bare feet into a small cranny, feeling pain burst through her sole as she sliced it open.

Stretching upwards as slowly as she could not to unbalance herself, she burned her anxiety by yelling, "I've got you, you son of a bitch," to the ceiling as loudly as she could.

Her fingers wiggled into the small opening around the edge of the trap door.

"Sugar?" someone—Jackson!—shouted and footsteps thundered above her.

"Wait," she yelled, but it was too late. The trapdoor thundered down on her, dislodging her with a smash as two hundred pounds of man and the door bashed down on her and they all tumbled down the slide, ending up in a horrible pile at the bottom.

She heard the trapdoor snap shut and couldn't help but moan in defeat. "I was so close."

Jackson rolled off her. "What the hell just happened?"

"The floor has another trapdoor," she said into the darkness. Where had her flashlight gone? She felt around the mattress, figuring if it had been dropped on the ground, she would have heard it hitting.

"How long have you been down here?" he asked, sitting up and seeming to do a full body check as he patted himself down for injuries.

She looked at the glowing hands of her watch. "A little over two hours."

"Ouch. There's no way out?"

"Yeah, there is. I was just trying to climb the slide for a challenge." She didn't mean to be sarcastic, but really did he think she was in a dungeon for fun?

"Ooooh, someone has the grumpies," he said, his voice full of mirth.

"Are you lying on my flashlight?" she asked, backing away from an extreme desire to show him what grumpy looked like.

"Not that I feel." He clicked on his own. "But I still have mine." He ran the light along the walls. "What is this place?" He climbed to his feet, so strong he didn't need his hands to rise.

Jackson Wright was in super shape in a muscle-bound, super-hero kind of way. She should work out more. Maybe then she would have climbed the slide like a champ.

"I have no idea. But it's just us, the mattress and the rug that came down with me in here." She hissed when she touched the cut on the bottom of her feet.

The beam highlighted her wound. "Ouch," he said in sympathy.

"Yeah." She dabbed at the small cut with her sock.

He sat and took the sock from her, holding pressure,

his hands gentle. "This should stop bleeding in a moment. We'll put something on it when we get out of here."

"What is wrong with this place? It's been designed by a madman." It made no sense. Why would they have a trapdoor here in the Admin Building?

"It sort-of made sense they had a trapdoor at the speakeasy. They could use it in a magic show or something like that."

"Yeah and I could see someone leaving it unsecured, even though they have to have rules in place to prevent that, but this is an office building."

"The rug was over it?" Jackson met her gaze while still holding her foot.

It was a very intimate thing. She didn't think anyone but her massage therapist had touched her feet before. It kind of weirdly turned her on. Who knew she had some sort of foot fetish thing going? Jackson was teaching her all kinds of inner secrets about herself. Too bad they were secrets she wished would stay hidden. "Yeah. I swear I could hear someone calling to me from the doorway on the far side of the room. Or maybe I didn't. I'm starting to second guess myself." She gently took her foot back from him, figuring she needed some distance. "Why did you come looking for me?"

He grinned a little sheepishly. "I came back for the radios."

"The radios," she said, slapping a hand to her forehead. How had she forgotten them? Usually they didn't use them unless actively filming, but this time, they'd packed a ton of them because cellphones didn't work here.

"Yeah, I was going to give one to Cindy so she could call me when she needed help."

"Cindy. Crap!" She rested her face in her hands. "I forgot all about her. I'm going to be fired." Here she was, trapped and useless, with contestants running amok all over the park with only Russ to herd them. Herding was not Russ' strength.

Jackson peeled her hands down. "Sugar, this is an insane situation. You're doing the best you can. Don't beat yourself up."

His voice was so compassionate and kind, she leaned in to kiss him before she fully thought it out. She only knew she needed comfort and he was offering it to her on such a soul-deep level, she couldn't resist.

His lips were warm and soft and wonderful, just like she knew they would be.

He curled a hand around the back of her head and drew her even closer, pulling her into his lap. And what had been comforting turned into something else entirely, morphing into red hot passion, the likes of which she'd never felt before. It started in the pit of her stomach and radiated out like a live wire running through her. She'd wanted him since they'd ridden the elevator down together only hours ago. It made no sense, but for this moment, she didn't care. His touch burned her insides and made her heart race. Straddling him, she rose so she could get a better angle on his mouth, letting her tongue explore him.

Oh my God in Heaven.

His smell wrapped around her, the cedarwood rich and the lime tangy, filling her head. She knew she'd never encounter those scents again without thinking of him.

Somewhere a small warning bell rang, but she ignored it as she shifted to better settle her jean clad sex against the bulge of his manhood. Just touching him like this made her whole body shiver.

His hands ran up and down her back, both comforting and caressing. Then they rested on her hips, dragging her closer.

She'd never wanted a man like she wanted this one.

Leaving his lips behind, she scraped her teeth on the skin of his ear lobe, enjoying the soft growl he let out, while her fingers worked the buttons on his shirt. He'd rolled up the sleeves and ditched his jacket long ago, and changed into jeans, which hugged his hips in all the right places.

He shrugged out of his shirt and stripped her t-shirt over her head. "Oh yes," he said reverent in the dim shadows created by his flashlight, which had fallen beside them unnoticed.

The chill air on her nakedness almost brought her out of her fugue, but then he tipped her breasts out of the cups of her bra and captured one with his mouth, while the other nipple hardened under his gently twisting fingers.

"Please," she begged, not even sure what she was asking for, except more of this feeling which ate its way through her body like exquisite torture.

He gave her what she wanted, easily shifting their positions so she lay beneath him.

This is totally dumb, some small part of her mind warned.

She didn't care. She wanted this and her malfunctioning brain didn't let her focus enough to stand up and walk away. *Although I'm trapped here.*

That was a lame excuse and she knew it.

Wetness flooded her sex and she wantonly twined her legs around his hips and rubbed herself against his raging erection, enjoying the moan that escaped him.

He ate at her mouth for a moment, then undid her jeans and jerked the tight fabric down her hips. She arched to help him, approving when he swept her panties away as well. Then he settled between her thighs and ran his perfect mouth along her right hip. Fingers slipped on the wetness, sliding inside the lips of her sex to find her clit.

She arched into him when he hit the right spot, trying to gentle her hands, which were buried deep in his hair.

His mouth licked along the line of where her underwear would naturally fall, way too far away from where she needed him to be.

"Jackson," she moaned, needing so much more.

"Ask me," he demanded.

"I—" she wasn't sure she had the words.

"I want to hear it," he said, licking along her left hipbone.

"Please, I would like you to go down on me," she gasped, immediately embarrassed and thrilled she'd demanded something she usually only enjoyed if a partner offered. How many times had that meant the opportunity passed her by?

"Gladly," he said, and ran his tongue in one, long, glorious swipe.

"Oh yes," she whispered, enjoying it so much more than she ever had before.

He repeated the gesture, his hands clamping her hips to the mattress so she couldn't move. She had to lie there and enjoy it. Heaven.

Then he picked up speed, one finger sliding easily inside her and the change in pressure combined with being filled had her soaring over the edge, shaking in both relief and the agony that it was over way too soon.

Jackson rose to lay beside her, pulling her body half on top of his into an embrace that made her feel cherished.

As her breathing quieted, she listened to his. She ran her hand along perfect washboard abs, feeling the layers of muscle. Enjoying his body in the aftermath.

"Thank you," she said, grateful he'd easily brought her to orgasm, when sometimes it had been so hard for her. It wasn't that she didn't want to come, she oh-so did. It was just that sometimes it had been almost impossible for her to let go and get there.

"You're welcome," he said, a hint of a growl in his voice letting her know he was still majorly turned on.

"Say it," she whispered, feeling that turnabout was fair play.

"Please take my cock in your mouth, Sugar sweet," he said, tipping her face up for a kiss.

"I thought you'd never ask," she purred, the power

over this man turning her on all over again.

She unbuttoned his jeans and he helped her pull them over his hips.

In the half-light, she could barely see him, but it was enough. He was so big, but that shouldn't have surprised her. He was big all over. She ran her tongue over the head of his cock, collecting the bead of salty come that had collected there.

"Oh yes," he mimicked her. Or maybe he just felt what she had. Anticipation so great, it almost overwhelmed her.

Then she ran her mouth along one side then the other of him, enjoying the velvet over rock hard that was so manly. For this moment, he was hers.

She set a pace that was slow and steady, letting him squirm and tremble with the slow speed of it.

When he came, it was unexpected for both of them. "Sugar," he moaned, holding onto her shoulders while his body pumped and shivered, so at her mercy, she felt as if she owned the world.

"You are amazing." He hauled her up beside him, placed a sweet kiss on her lips and promptly fell asleep.

Sugar rested her head on his wide, muscled chest, the smooth, warm skin soft over the hard. Under her hand, she could feel his heartbeat, slow and steady as he slept, his breathing deep and calm.

It would have relaxed her if the thought that this had been a colossal fuck up didn't rise up and bite her in the ass. She might not truly feel as if she'd messed up now, but she knew in an hour or two or whenever someone got them out of this hole, it would be a major deal.

She closed her eyes and inhaled his scent. Cedarwood and lime comforted her. It must be his aftershave, if men still used that stuff. Or his deodorant. It smelled perfect on him. Of course it would. She wouldn't have succumbed to him if he hadn't smelled amazing.

This would have been easier if she didn't like him so much. He was genuinely a good guy, which in her experience was weird for someone as hot as he was. Hot people tended to be self-obsessed and narcissistic.

Less than wonderful in bed.

Adding to his charm, he was handy as hell on a set. He had spent the day wiring cameras, for God's sake. No other Bachelors in the history of Bachelors wired cameras or did first aid or seemed to roll with punches like Jackson Wright. Nothing flustered him.

She sighed and rolled over to stare up at the pitch black of their prison. He followed her to his side and slipped a thigh over hers, while one arm tucked her close. She resisted the urge to groan in frustration. Her last boyfriend had not been a cuddler, so she promised herself she'd never date someone again who didn't like to cuddle.

She realized then that the Bachelor, a member of the *cast*, was her dream man. She'd been looking for him every-where and here he was. The only person on the planet Earth who was off limits.

She resisted the urge to scream in frustration.

Jackson knew Sugar was awake by how stiffly she laid under his arm. Her body was like a live wire ready to snap. This did not bode well for the coming conversation, but he was a man who didn't like to put off unpleasant things, so he said, "You okay?"

He was pretty sure she was about to tell him they'd made a terrible mistake. Since they had, he figured she had a point. Not that he regretted what had just happened. He didn't and he'd be annoyed if she did. Because Sugar scream-ing his name had been the best thing that had ever happened to him.

"No, Jackson, I'm not okay," she said, a growl in her

tone.

A little shiver of lust shook through him, but he stamped it out. Now was *not* the time to try to get his sexy on. Sugar was dead serious and he might end up losing a limb if he wasn't careful. "I understand," he said, since he did.

She wiggled out from under him, and while he didn't restrain her, he didn't help her either, allowing himself to enjoy the full body brush she inadvertently gave him. Man oh man, she was all woman. Curves that went on for miles, full perfect breasts, and a rear end he could stare at for hours. Sugar was perfect on every level.

"I do not need to tell you this was a contract breach on your part and an offense I could be fired for on mine."

When she put it like that, it did seem dire. "Okay," he said, because even so, he didn't regret it.

She wrapped her arms around her legs, a motion he could feel more than see since his flashlight had died sometime during their love play. "You are supposed to be choosing a fiancée. That is the whole point of this show."

"I know it is. I choose you," he said, feeling like in for a penny, in for a pound. As far as he was concerned, he had come here to find someone and he had.

A little part of him whispered about his dreams to get back in space. Well, he'd just need to talk Hank Carson into making Sugar one of the contestants. Then he'd choose Sugar and it would all work out. Problem solved.

Something told him Sugar wouldn't like this idea, so he wisely kept silent about it. He'd just have to sneak in, call Hank, and lay the idea out to him.

"Whoa," Sugar said, and even in the pitch dark, he could feel her holding out her hands to stop him. "You can NOT choose me. I am NOT a choice." She scrambled around in the dark for her clothes.

"Well, that's unfortunate because I have chosen you." He laid back, feeling her shirt under him. She wasn't going to escape this uncomfortable conversation. Not that she could escape. They were locked in here together.

"That's impossible."

"Nothing is impossible," he said. It was his personal motto and he was sticking to it.

"I am not a contestant. Your choices are twelve women who have been handpicked for you. I am not one of the twelve." She laid back to drag on her panties.

Jackson located and tried a flashlight that must be her lost one so he could watch, rolling onto his side. "We can have Hank add you to the list," he suggested, unable to resist trying his idea out on her even though he'd just decided to hide it from her.

She gave him an icy stare over the jeans she'd just stuck her feet into. "I am *not* a contestant. I am crew."

There was something in the way she said that, as if he'd stepped on her pride. "What's so bad about being a contestant?" he asked, annoyance flickering through him.

"Jackson, this is my job. A job I have trained at for years, making nothing for money, essentially an indentured slave." She wiggled the jeans up over her hips.

God, she was an amazingly beautiful woman. He blinked to clear his head.

"Do you know why I would work for peanuts?" She secured her bra over her beautiful chest.

"Tell me," he said, fascinated. He'd worked for nothing for years, but then, he owned a space station. If it hadn't ended up as space trash, it would have been one hell of a cool asset.

"Where's my shirt?" She found it under him and yanked one end.

He reluctantly raised his butt so she could rescue it.

She narrowed her eyes. "Were you sitting on it on purpose?"

"Me?" he asked, blinking innocently at her.

She rolled her eyes. "I worked for peanuts because that's what you do to get to the big bucks. You put in your time at the bottom so you can make it to the top. That's how it goes in show business."

He nodded. If he had been able to sell Genesis III, he would have been rich for life. He knew all about working for nothing for a big payoff in the end.

"I become a contestant, I lose everything. All my hard work. Gone." She flicked her fingers. "Poof."

"That's not true." It couldn't be true.

"It is. This is my big shot. My *one* and *only* chance at being Head Wrangler. If I don't pull this off, I'll never be hired by anyone else again. I'll be associated with a failure. That's the kiss of death."

"But surely Hank Carson will hire you?"

"Hank is dating Lynette, who is currently pregnant with his child. They are getting married after Atlantis wraps. He is not ever hiring another Head Wrangler again unless Lynette steps down." She dragged her shirt over her head, the one that designated her as crew. "I must have a successful show. This is my one big opportunity."

Suddenly, all his plans to corner Hank to talk him into letting Sugar be his choice came crashing down. He liked Sugar way too much to cause her to lose her chance. "Fuck," he said, flopping back on the mattress and staring at the trapdoor above them.

"You see why I can't let anything derail me, no matter how I feel about you."

"Yeah." He did see. Here he was, hanging out with the woman of his dreams, the taste of her still on his lips and he finally understood he'd never have her. She really was off limits.

He was going to have to choose one of the others. The thought had exactly zero appeal to him. He wanted Sugar, but that was just too damn bad.

"Of course, if I don't get out of here, it won't matter, because I'm going to end up losing complete control of everything that's going on up there." She sounded so forlorn, he ached to comfort her.

He could try to push her into changing her mind, but that would only leave them at odds in the end. He knew that deep in his soul. She had to come to him.

Well, the least he could do was help her, now that he'd decided to let her go. He sat up and pulled on his own clothes. "Then let's get out of here."

Sugar froze. "Are you telling me you could get out of here this whole time?"

"No, but I believe I can do anything I set my mind to, so if we need to get out of here, we'll get out of here."

"I see," she said, doubtfully.

"I'm not bragging, I'm just stating fact."

"If that's so, why didn't you get us out of here sooner?"

"Why would I have wanted to? I was with the only person on the show I wanted to be with."

"Jackson," she said, and he knew she was about to launch back into a speech about how they couldn't be together, blah blah.

He held up a hand. "I get it." He studied the slide. "I should be able to boost you so you can grab the top edge of the trapdoor."

"I'm not strong enough to pull myself up." She shrugged, looking a bit embarrassed. "I already tried and I don't have the upper body strength for that."

"Okay," he said.

"You aren't going to insist I try?"

"You know what you're capable of." He walked the outside of the room, running the flashlight along the walls.

"What are you doing?"

"Why would they put a room down here that goes nowhere?" he asked, answering her question with a question.

She stood and turned a circle looking at the walls. "I don't know."

"I mean it would cost a fortune to dig this basement

down here to sit empty, right?" He completed his circle but still ran the flashlight along the walls around them, thinking. "The other tunnels and storage rooms made sense. They probably stock a ton and store it so they can keep inventory for the high season readily available. So why have this weird room to nowhere?"

"You're right. It makes no sense."

He took another pass around the room, this time knocking on the walls at short intervals. Almost no sound came from his knuckles against the rock... until he got to the far wall. A hollow sound reverberated through the room. "Here."

He felt her move up behind him and passed her the light.

Then he took two steps back and slammed his left foot into the wall. The loafers they'd insisted he wear weren't as good as his boots, but they still slammed straight through the thin board that was covering the entrance to a doorway. Which was great until his shoe connected with the closed door behind it. "Son of a..." He hopped a few times as the pain reverberated up his leg and into his brain stem.

"Oh my God. I never even thought to check the walls. Why didn't I think to check the walls?" She passed by him to reach through for the door knob. "Locked."

He finished hopping and limped over. "That's okay. I can pick it." He knelt down on his good leg and pulled out his picks, ignoring the throb in his foot. Sugar might not be a possibility but for some reason he didn't want to look too closely at, he wanted her to think of him as a hero.

"Smashing down fake walls *and* picking locks," she said, with enough awe he couldn't help the stab of pride.

"Maybe," he said, sliding in the picks and feeling for the tumblers. He was getting better at this. "Got it." The tiny click of the lock opening was more something he felt than could see.

The door swung wide on perfectly oiled hinges.

CHAPTER NINE

Sugar had to admit that Jackson Wright was amazing in many, many areas, not the least of which was in bed. Maybe it was good they hadn't had actual sex-sex, because it might have caused her to have a heart attack and die from the pleasure, or worse, spoil sex with anyone else for the rest of her life.

Setting all that aside, she focused on their current crisis. They needed to get out of the tunnels so she could check on the contestants. She was super worried they had been unsupervised for so long. A simple drive-by would do, maybe distribute the box of snacks and some water, then cruise to Mike's Magical Knick Knacks to call Hank.

He needed to speed everything up and get here pronto. Atlantis had turned dangerous. Until then, every person, including contestants, were going to be assigned a radio until Hank and the rest of the crew arrived. The last thing she needed was to lose someone permanently. That would be a huge black mark on her wrangler resume and would have her in therapy from the guilt for the rest of her life.

"I think I'm beginning to understand how to navigate down here," Jackson said, his deep, melodious voice doing things to her insides. Lynette had said that on the space station, she'd to ban him from using the announcement system, because just the sound of him made women shiver.

Sugar wished he wasn't so wonderful.

Well, she was just going to have to drag her big girl panties up, slap a smile on her face, and do her J-O-B. And why was she angsting about him, *again?* "I'm glad one of us knows where we're going. I am still completely turned around."

"I think these dots correlate to sections of the park." He pointed at the corner of an upcoming intersection.

She ran her light along the wall and found a yellow circle painted about halfway up. On the other corner, there was a red dot. "The map was color coded." But she couldn't remember now what sections were what and her clipboard was sitting in her golf cart. She thought International Street was in the red section.

Jackson must have thought that too, because he turned right and led her along, past the doorways to the storage areas and soon enough to the left-hand turn that took them up the short flight of stairs into the speakeasy basement.

"Thank God," she said, wanting to sit down and order a beer, but there was no rest for the wicked. "I need to go back to the Admin Building. I feel like I've been going in circles all day." Probably because she had been. She should race down to her golf cart, but she was just too tired.

"Why go back there?" Jackson stared at her as if she were crazy.

"I have to check the contestants and I'm not walking, so I have to pick up the golf cart." And she needed to do that now. "Knowing my luck, they'll all be stuck in a well by now."

"I doubt there are any wells here," Jackson pointed out, his tone reasonable.

"Can you guarantee that?"

"I can't guarantee anything about this place but that it's unpredictable."

"Exactly." She left the alcohol that was calling her name behind and stepped into the street, preparing for the long journey to get her cart. While they'd been gone, the light from the surface had completely faded, leaving only small pools of illumination from weak bulbs hanging from lamp posts every few feet along International Street.

She added to her growing list for Hank the fact they were going to have to turn on more lights down here, cost be dammed.

Jackson stopped her with a hand on her arm. "I don't think we should split up."

She didn't either, but what she wanted and what had to happen were two different things, so she moved her body away, needing to have some separation so she could think. She'd made a mistake, but wasn't going to make another. "We shouldn't be alone anymore." They would need to set some ground rules. No touching, being number one.

"Sugar," Jackson said, stepping close, his voice so deep and intense, a piece of her melted. The way he said her name, the feel of his voice as it thrummed through her.

"Sugar," Russ called, his tone far, far from hot, as he saved her—from what, she didn't know.

In the distance, a ragtag group ambled into view as they came out of the darkness.

She moved away from Jackson to meet them, thanking her lucky stars that the cast hadn't caught them in some sort of embrace. Rule number one, no touching. Or wait. Rule number one was no being alone together. Rule number two was no touching. Although she wouldn't need rule number two if she followed rule number one.

"Did you guys end up with some great selfies?" she asked, pitching her voice into enthusiastic wrangler mode. She had a show to manage and she wasn't going to let things go south as long as she was breathing.

Instead of excitement, they groaned, attesting to the fact they had not had fun.

"Do you realize how big this place is?" Jillian asked.

Sugar hadn't really thought about it.

"You sent us to every corner of the park," Lena groused.

Sugar had done exactly that, on purpose.

"My heels are completely raw," Raven snarled, then pulled off one tennis shoe to show her.

Sugar stopped herself from pointing out that wearing socks with tennis shoes was done for a reason. This wasn't the time to tell Lena it was her fault for having blisters when Sugar had purposely death marched them around the park to buy herself time.

"And we're *starving*," Andi said, her tone a mix of pleading and a whine.

"There should be food in the apartment kitchens for you," Sugar said, meeting Jackson's gaze and almost melting in relief when he nodded that he'd taken care of putting it there. God, he was reliable, a trait she always found sexy in a man. "This way," she said, herding them back toward the apartments.

"Hi Jackson," Jillian cooed as she passed him.

"Russ, could you get a case of water from the warehouse and bring it up to the ladies? And we'll need to pass out radios." Sugar didn't miss Russ' grumpy look as she led the women through the Employee's Only door. She understood he wanted a break. Hell, she did too, but no one got a break until every one of the cast was in their rooms, safely locked away for the night. *Suck it up, buttercup,* she thought to Russ, but also to her own inner whiner who just wanted to lay down and try again tomorrow.

"Radios? What radios?" Russ asked.

"They're down with the golf carts. I'll show you." Jackson put a hand on Russ' shoulder and swept him in the right direction, since he was still allowed to touch Russ.

He knew Sugar was right. They had to disengage. He just didn't like it.

"I don't want to go get water." Russ had clearly had

enough. He was limping and his camera was dangling from his hands instead of up at the ready to film.

"We fell through another trap door," Jackson said to distract him, wanting to pick up the pace but couldn't when he realized how badly Russ was limping. He wished there was a steak dinner in one of the crates down in the warehouse. He could really use lots of food right now, but he hadn't seen anything but MREs, the stamp on them proclaiming them old army surplus. He wondered if there were any frozen meat in the freezers at the speakeasy. One of the few things he missed in space was the ability to cook, since he enjoyed it and enjoyed eating a good meal even more.

"Yeah?" The fact they'd run into more trouble seemed to give Russ the lift he needed.

"Yeah. In the Admin Building when Sugar was looking for Barbara. She fell right through with the rug she'd been walking on, then like an idiot, I fell in when I was searching for her."

"Not such an idiot since this place is dark as a tomb," Russ said as they went around the corner to descend the hill to the Administration area, leaving behind the cutesy iron street lamps that had been giving off a weak glow on International Street, plunging them into darkness.

Jackson's flashlight only illuminated a short distance in front of them. Luckily, he knew this route by heart, but maybe he should pick up a couple more flashlights from the warehouse. "We'll each grab a golf cart and drive it back up."

"Why'd you leave them down here?"

"We fell into the tunnels and ended up coming out at the speakeasy."

"This place is amazing," Russ said, in a tone that said he really thought it was.

"That's one way of looking at it. The other might be that it's dangerous as hell." Jackson peeled off to go to the warehouse. The radios and extra water were still on his cart. "I'm going to pick up another couple flashlights. You want one?"

"Sure." Russ followed him. "You don't think some-one was purposely trying to trap you guys, do you?"

Jackson swept his light along the crates until he found the right one, but then paused to really think through what Russ was asking. "If they are, they haven't done that great of a job since we keep escaping."

"True. Although what if they weren't trying to trap us, but rather trying to stop filming? Because if that was their goal, they have actually succeeded." Russ paused, then continued, "Although they haven't counted on Hank Carson. He'll figure out a way to film if it kills him."

Jackson pulled out a couple extra flashlights, handing one to Russ, who immediately turned it on and peered into the closest crate.

Now that was an interesting thought. "Yeah," he agreed, really considering it. "If the goal was to stop filming, then that has certainly happened." And at the perfect time, too, so no immediate rescue could come and the rest of the cast wasn't able to join them. "But why would anyone want to stop filming?"

"They don't. I'm sure we're just falling through the trapdoors that someone forgot to secure. Those weren't built recently, so they had nothing to do with us. They've been here for a long time," Russ said his tone saying he'd clearly moved on.

"So why did you bring it up?"

"Because it would be cool if they had."

Jackson shook his head, because he didn't think it would be cool at all.

"Since we're down here, there is more camera equipment I need. Can you carry one of these bags while I get the other?" He fished out a backpack from the crate and handed it over.

"Sure." Jackson put it on, still stuck on how perfect things were going if the point was to delay filming. "Are we only able to film down here for a certain length of time?"

"Two weeks here. That was already tight as hell, but when it comes to Hank Carson, nothing is impossible." Russ put on his own backpack. "Even now, when he arrives, he'll crush things into the remaining time and bump out the time filming on the surface."

"Yeah, but filming *has* been halted." Looking at everything that had happened to them, could it be someone really had closed the door in the tunnels? And Sugar had said she heard someone calling her when she fell in the Admin Building. He hadn't thought about it again, because he'd been distracted by what had happened between them.

"If anyone thinks they can disrupt filming, they don't know Hank. He'll just film what he can here, build a set of this place back at the studio and fake the rest."

They walked to the golf carts. "I don't think you're kidding."

"Hank is the master at making bad situations into gold. I'm under a non-disclosure—"

"As am I," Jackson reminded him.

"True," Russ said excitedly. "Then I can tell you that's what Hank did for Space Bachelor. After we had to evacuate, he faked the whole rest of the show in the studio. It was genius."

From down the street, something snapped and both men turned their flashlights toward the noise, finding someone bent over lifting something from the ground.

"Niles?" Jackson guessed, not completely sure, because the older man was dressed all in black and hard to see in the darkness.

Niles straightened and raised a hand to block Russ' light from his eyes. "I heard people talking and came to investigate."

"Where have you been?" Russ asked. "We've been looking for you everywhere."

"I must maintain the systems which are keeping us

safe," Niles said in his rusty voice.

Jackson would love to see how this place operated. He'd bet it would be very similar to a space station.

"We were told there would be people to assist us." Russ sounded less like Russ and more like a real, grown up professional.

"This place is very fragile," Niles said, his voice prim. "Lay people don't realize what it takes to keep this park running. Currently, we have a large issue with the air handler which I'm attempting to fix. It's quite involved."

"I would love to see the workings of Atlantis," Jackson said, wondering if he could finesse a tour.

Niles rose up to his full, considerable height. "Guests are not allowed in the maintenance areas. They are strictly off limits." Then without another word, he shuffled past them, not going up the hill toward International Street but past the amphitheater to a section of the park Jackson had not been to.

Curious, he vowed that tomorrow he'd take a golf cart and see what was down there.

"That guy is seriously weird," Russ said.

"Agreed."

"I hope he gets the air handler working."

"Me too." Because that would seriously suck to be suddenly out of breathable air. A thrill raced through him at the thought of the challenge to fix something like that. It would be just like working in space, his life on the line, pins and needles of fear and adrenaline coursing through him.

As he climbed in Sugar's golf cart, which still had the box of snacks on the front seat, he noticed her clipboard and picked it up. Studying the map, he saw he was right. The International Street area was coded red. This area was yellow. The area with all the rides was blue. The theater area where they'd come down was green. The area Niles had been going to had no color at all, but was rather drawn with nothing in it, left empty on the map.

"We going or what?" Russ called.

"Or what," Jackson muttered, but started the golf cart.

CHAPTER TEN

The contestants sat in the lounge area of their apartments, well and truly pissed. Sugar had finally fed them, but that had only seemed to give them the strength to vent. They were so mad, she was worried she was about to have an uprising on her hands. She supposed this was when she earned her real money, but she was exhausted and hungry and just wanted to go to bed.

"You're right," she agreed, knowing people loved to be right and she admitted she hadn't really taken into account just how big Atlantis was when she'd made the scavenger hunt. She'd picked the furthest places on the map to keep them busy the longest. "That was too much. Tomorrow for our outing, I'll assign you all golf carts." Hank would have kittens, but he wasn't here to over-rule her and she wasn't about to ask him for permission ahead of time.

"Okay, then," said Lena, a bit sulkily because it was clear she hadn't fully gotten her grievances out of her system, but who didn't like to drive a golf cart?

Sugar knew sometimes people had to vent, but she didn't have the patience for it right now. She was tired and wanted a drink. A strong one, the kind that gave her a full body shiver after she took a sip. "Look, we're all exhausted. This has been a hell of a day and tomorrow will be long too. I know this wasn't what any of us signed up for," an understatement of massive proportions, "but we're going to need to dig deep and come together."

"We want to know when they're going to rescue us," Jillian demanded.

"Yeah when?" Raven asked. The other two nodded their heads.

"You know we came down in the elevator because all the submarines are in dry dock for their yearly maintenance. They are bringing a sub out of dry dock now and will come for us." Sugar knew there was no use hiding the bad news. "It will take another day before they arrive."

This news went over worse than she expected because there was a sudden shift in the mood of the room. What had been grumpiness and frustration suddenly shifted into tangible anger.

"We have another *day* down here before help arrives?" Andi asked, her mouth hanging open.

"We don't need help," Sugar pointed out, keeping her voice calm and reasonable. "Everyone is fine."

"Tell that to Cindy," Lena grumbled.

Sugar raised her voice to talk over her. "We just need to keep busy until the rest of the cast and crew arrives."

Jillian narrowed her eyes. "Keep busy. Was that what you were doing with us today? Busy work?"

Uh oh. Sugar scrambled to smooth things over. "Absolutely not. Those pictures will be all over the promotions and social media, as well as on the show intros." She would now need to get Hank to put them on the opening show credits. There had better be some good shots.

"You were trying to keep us out of the way while you did," Lena paused as she struggled to think what Sugar could possibly be up to, since the cast never understood exactly what went in to filming these shows. Then she came up with, "*whatever.*"

"I was working on trying to coordinate with the park employees." Sugar almost let slip she'd fallen through the floor and had been stuck in a dungeon, but then thought better of it. The last thing she needed was panic. That was the one emotion that was almost impossible to recover from. Anger wasn't unusual on a reality TV set. She could handle this.

"Coordinate? What the hell does that mean?" Jillian asked.

They weren't going to be distracted, no matter how hard Sugar tried. She was going to have to do something big to regain control. There was really only one trick she had up her sleeve, but for a moment she resisted it, frantically trying to come up with another option. A spa day? Wouldn't work down here since there wasn't a spa. A chance to leave confinement? Nope. Maybe she could offer them guaranteed spots on *Paradise*? But if she did that, she would never have control of them again. With Paradise guaranteed, they'd go completely off the rails.

"What were you guys thinking by not having another safety route out of here? That has to be some sort of contract breach not to keep us safe." The calculation in Jillian's eyes was scary. She was going to make trouble of massive proportions and sweep the other women along with her.

"You are completely safe," Sugar said, her voice not betraying her growing concern at how quickly things had gone out of control. Jillian was right. They shouldn't have come down here without a second way out. Sugar shouldn't have sent them all over the park on a death march. That had been a huge miscalculation. Of course, the cast had signed away their rights to sue when they did all the pre-filming paperwork, but pointing that out would only make them angrier. "Since you have all been so patient and understanding, as a special thank you for all of you who had to go through this, I'm going to have a group date tomorrow with the four of you and the Bachelor." Sugar could almost feel Hank flipping out wherever he was on the surface. He would be enraged when he heard she was violating one of his biggest rules, but Hank wasn't here and Sugar had to do what she had to do to regain control.

Jillian blinked, her mouth opening and closing as it quickly came to her what a massive advantage this was for the four of them.

"Well, okay then," Raven said, one hand going to her hair as if she were already thinking about what she was going to do with it for the date.

"Fantastic," Sugar said, standing to make her escape while she still had things under control. "I'll let you all go to bed," she made a shooing motion with her hands to start them on their way to their rooms. "And will meet you here at 10AM with all the details." All she wanted to do was fall face down on her covers and sleep for a year, but now she'd have to figure out where to have the group date and get Russ to set up the cameras.

On her way out, Sugar made sure Cincy had everything she needed and went to call Hank. She looked at her watch. It was ten o'clock and she wanted nothing more than to crawl into her bed, but something had to be done about Atlantis not providing the two employees they'd promised. If she was going to put on this extra group date, she'd need access to somewhere to do it. She was thinking about the Ferris Wheel, but currently there was no one to operate the ride.

Where was Barbara anyway? She could have sworn someone called her before she'd fallen through the trapdoor, but if Barbara was in the Admin Building, why hadn't she come to Sugar's aid? Sugar figured she must have been hearing things, probably because this place was making her crazy.

How was she supposed to be successful if she kept falling through trapdoors and getting locked in the tunnels? A large piece of her wanted to go home, but since that wasn't an option on so many levels, she stomped over to Mike's Magical Knick Knacks ready to do battle with Hank.

Her hand on the doorknob, she heard an engine and paused. It turned out to be two engines as Jackson and Russ came around the corner from picking up the golf carts. She waited for them, wanting her radio before she had another accident.

They pulled up beside her. "What's wrong?" Jackson asked as he dismounted.

She shook her head, not in the mood for another example of the unwanted connection between them. She'd waited her whole life for a man who cared about how she was feeling and who could recognize when she needed support and here she finally got what she wanted with the exact wrong person. "Russ, we're going to have a group date tomorrow. I need you to wire a new location."

Russ raised his eyebrows at her but wisely kept his mouth shut about how it was a bad idea, thereby saving his life. Great. A second man in her life who understood her. "Where were you thinking about having it?"

"Is my clipboard in there?" she asked, feeling naked without it.

Jackson handed it to her. "Those paint dots in the tunnels do coincide with the sections of the park as we thought."

She nodded absently, barely listening since she planned never to end up in the tunnels ever again. Running blindly into rooms was a thing of the past. The electricity bill be damned, she was turning on lights everywhere and moving slowly from now on.

The back of the map had a list of locations, all broken up helpfully by food, rides, attractions, and games. "I already have a games day planned for them, so we can't do that." Although she was tempted to steal the idea and let them all have a turn with the Bachelor doing the ring toss and shooting wooden targets, then pick a winner. But stealing from Peter to pay Paul was a terrible idea. She needed to come up with a new activity.

"I thought I wasn't allowed to see the contestants until the first evening?" Jackson asked unhelpfully from where he leaned against the front of her golf cart.

She spared a moment to shoot him a frown from

above her map. "The natives are restless. I have to give them a group date or there will be an uprising."

"Uh oh," Russ said, knowing she didn't use that term lightly. Five seasons ago, Lynette had ended up with women throwing plates and glasses at the crew and each other for a very long ten minutes in protest of the crew accidentally sending the same people on the second group date who'd gone on the first. Things only calmed down when the cupboards were bare.

"Yeah. They were disgruntled I marched them all around the park today."

"I'm totally on their side about that. I'm going to be sore for a week." Russ hobbled out of his golf cart toward her as if to illustrate his point.

"Yeah, I may have gotten a little over zealous in picking my destinations." Although she'd wanted to keep them occupied and out of her hair, which she'd done.

"A date huh? Like a group date for the four of them?" Jackson sounded about as excited as a patient before hemorrhoid surgery.

"I figure we can use the footage later and mix it in. Maybe this could be the first group date we were supposed to have after the first mixer." She was grasping at straws and she knew it.

Russ opened his mouth, then closed it.

"Just say it and get it over with," she said with a sigh.

"Hank isn't going to like it," Russ said in a rush.

"I know." Hank was going to be furious with her. She wasn't going to kill Russ for stating the obvious. Besides, who would film the date? She'd tried her hand once at filming and she was terrible at it. The whole time she filmed, she'd get distracted and end up filming something else entirely like her own feet. "Moving on, where should we have the date?"

"Can we use any of the rides if we don't have someone from the park to run them for us?" Having gotten the Hank warning out of his system, Russ moved on as instructed.

"I don't think so unless we locate one of the staff members here. Maybe we could get a cooking group date going?" But she had planned to stay away from cooking on this show. The audience just thought it was okay, not tons of fun like most of the other dates.

"It would be better if we had some rides we could use," Russ said. "It would be more interesting visually. Too bad we can't take out the submarine."

"All the subs are in dry dock," she said absently, discarding the mud wrestling idea because they had no way to make mud here in the bubble.

"No, not the subs that take customers from the surface to the park. There is a ride that takes people around the bubble. It just circles the park on a track. I could get amazing footage from out there."

"That's still a ride." It was a cool idea. "Let's put that as one of the first dates when we finally locate staff members who can help us."

Russ grinned, a rare sign of happiness. "Sweet."

"We could do golf cart races," Jackson said, his face deadpan.

Russ' grin stretched wider. "Perfect suggestion."

Jackson blinked. "I was joking."

She tapped one finger to her lips, thinking. It wasn't a bad idea. It would have action, adventure, drama, all the pieces. "Let's sleep on it. I'm going to go try to get Hank on the phone. Lynette was supposed to be working on ideas to keep the contestants amused, so she might have come up with something."

"You're going to tell Hank about the group date?" Russ eyes were huge.

"Of course not. I'm going to tell him about it when he gets here and sees for himself what a complete cluster this whole thing has been."

"Seriously, Sugar, you have to tell him."

She knew Russ would pester her forever until she

agreed. "Okay. I'll tell him right now," she lied. She turned away, already wanting to get the conversation over with so she could go to bed. "I'll see you both tomorrow. Six AM will come quickly, so you should get some rest, Russ."

"You don't have to tell me twice." Russ hobbled toward the crew apartments.

"You should take Russ with you," Jackson said.

"No," she said, more tired than angry.

"Then—"

"No," she cut him off, too tired to fight. "Just, no." And she beat feet for the phone, not looking back. Yes, she agreed with him that it was better if they didn't split up, but she wasn't going to fall through a trapdoor in Mike's Magical Knick Knacks.

"Wait." Feet ran after her.

She turned, gearing up for a fight she just didn't have the energy to have.

"At least take a radio," he said, handing it to her.

She nodded and accepted the gift, noting he hadn't argued again with her, but had turned to go back up the street without needing to be asked. His muscular body was just as awesome to watch going as it was coming and she found herself a few moments later still standing in the same spot.

"Get a hold of yourself, girl," she whispered. Then turned on the radio and continued her mission. Not that she expected Hank to answer. He was probably sleeping like a baby in some cushy bed while she was here on the edge of a nervous breakdown. Still, she had to try.

Only when she dialed, Hank *did* answer. On the second ring, with a crisp, "Carson."

"It's Sugar," she said, suddenly dead tired and wanting to sit down. She hooked a foot around a nearby straight-backed chair leg and dragged it over.

"You okay?" he asked, sounding genuinely concerned.

"This place is dangerous, Hank." There was no reason

to beat around the bush about it. She fell into the chair in more of a collapse than a sit.

"What's happened?"

She had to force herself to tell him. "I fell through another trapdoor."

"*You* did? Where?"

"I'm fine. No need to worry I broke my arm or knocked my head," she said, annoyed he hadn't asked.

"That was rude of me. Are you hurt?"

Was she? Not really, more depressed because she'd somehow made an idiot's mistake falling for the talent. "Idiot," she murmured aloud.

"What?" Hank sounded startled.

"I'm not hurt, just exhausted." She held her head in her hand, supporting her elbow on the chair arm so she wouldn't topple into the floor.

"How did you get out?"

"I didn't return when I said I would and Jackson came to find me. I'd probably still be down there if he hadn't." She hastily changed the subject before he could ask her too many questions. "This place is dangerous, Hank. I know that sounds dramatic, but twice people have fallen into the basement tunnels unexpectedly."

"That is very strange. Where did it happen?"

"In the Admin Building when I went looking for Barbara. I fell into a room with no way out. I can't find her or any of the Atlantis staff, by the way."

"In the Admin Building? The stage made sense but why would they have a trapdoor in their offices?"

"Because this place is crackerjacks, that's why." Although he hadn't really been asking her. He'd just been talking out loud in his surprise. Well, they'd all been surprised by Atlantis and not in a good way. "I've seen Niles twice, but he's so weird, I hesitate to ask him to run the rides for us."

"Why are you trying to access the rides?"

Sugar geared up for a fight. "The women need things

to do. They are really angry they haven't been rescued yet."

"They don't need to be rescued. None of them were seriously hurt."

That wasn't exactly true, but she wasn't going to argue with him. "You know what I mean. They don't like that they're stuck down here and I don't blame them. Further, the scavenger hunt idea only made them angry." She took a calming breath, trying to stay on track. "Hank we need to get out of here. I'm starting to have a really bad feeling something is very off."

He sighed, the sound long and troubled. Not good. Not good at all. "I wish I could hurry things along, but the submarine they're sending was in several pieces for maintenance work when we asked for it. They are putting it back together as fast as they can. They've thrown every resource at it, I promise you. One more day and we'll be there."

"I'm going to have to do something with the cast. They are on the edge of uprising." She didn't say the last word lightly.

"Oh shit," Hank summarized perfectly. Uprising was one step away from imploding. Once a cast reached that stage, you might as well pack your gear because not even Hank could salvage things. "What can I do for you?"

"Find where Barbara or whomever is in charge down here is hiding. I need support from Atlantis staff pronto."

"Yeah, about that." Hank stopped, as if he had to structure the bad news.

Her stomach tightened. "What?" she asked, almost not wanting to hear.

"You're supposed to have Barbara and John helping you. I spoke with the park manager and he said no one named Niles works at Atlantis."

Icy fingers feathered up Sugar's spine, washing away her exhaustion. "Hank, there has to be someone named Niles because I've seen him twice. There has to be some sort of mistake." She tried to cling to the facts. Niles had been waiting for their elevator. "He knew when we were going to arrive and had the keys to all the buildings with him. He took us straight to our apartments."

"Well, according to the manager, he doesn't work there. And the manager hasn't been able to reach Barbara or John by landline either."

Panic threatened to overwhelm her as her mind tried to process the news, but she wasn't going to panic. She'd long ago learned that was the way to disaster. "What are you saying? That there is someone here who has taken over the park?"

"It does sound bad, I agree. The park manager is coming with me to get to the bottom of what's going on. I've decided not to bring the rest of the crew until I understand what's happening."

Her stomach fell. If Hank chose to delay filming in any way, then things were much worse than he'd told her. "Hank, your arrival is a long time from now. People have fallen through trapdoors. Russ could have been really hurt. *I* could have been really hurt." Of course, she hadn't been. Instead she'd made a terrible decision to have almost-sex with the Bachelor. Sugar jerked her mind away from that subject. She'd made a mistake, she was going to recover from it. Period. "Why do they even have trapdoors here, anyway? They must serve a purpose."

"I'll ask the park management."

"Fine," she said, because it really didn't matter. Right now, she needed to concentrate on the growing crisis. "How am I supposed to keep people safe from a madman?"

"I never said this Niles guy was a madman," Hank said in his 'don't panic' tone.

A bolt of annoyance speared through her. "Okay, so how would you describe him? Someone who has taken over the park, who has been impersonating the staff, and all the staff is mysteriously missing?"

Hank was silent.

"Yeah, exactly," she said, miffed, which on the whole was better than panicked.

"Listen, I'll be there on Thursday around eleven in the morning. You just have to keep everyone safe until then. Stay up by the apartments. Always move in twos. Keep people out of buildings you haven't explored yet."

"How am I going to do that?" she asked. "I'm only one woman and you know contestants need constant monitoring."

"You're Head Wrangler, Sugar. You'll figure it out." He paused. "And Sugar?"

"Yes?" Her head was spinning with this new information. Had someone locked the door to keep them lost in the tunnels? Had the trapdoor been a trap instead of a mistake? Everything that had happened so far took on a sinister outlook.

"Don't tell *anyone* this is happening. If you do, you'll just have panic on your hands. Not even Russ."

CHAPTER ELEVEN

The next morning, Jackson watched Sugar standing on the sidewalk outside of the cast apartments, instinctively knowing something had gone wrong. She was covering it like a professional, but there was a tightness in her face that said she was majorly stressed. He started to ask her what was wrong, but Russ was with them. He suspected this was part of Sugar's plan to keep them from fraternizing, but it made it hard for him to ask personal questions. Which he supposed was the point.

"I need you guys to start bringing up golf carts. We're going to have a race a little after 10 AM," she said, worry and stress washing off her in waves.

He wanted to step close, tip her chin up and ask her what was wrong. Give her a reassuring hug and tell her that between the two of them, they could work it out. "We're racing golf carts?" He wished he hadn't suggested it.

"We sure are," she said with false positivity, stepping into the road to point down to the ticket area. "We'll start down there and race to the end of International Street."

"That's going to be hard to film," Russ said, grumpy in the extreme. Shocking no one, it had turned out Russ wasn't a morning person.

Sugar whirled on him, obviously not in the mood for pushback. "Russ, you are the best cameraman in the business."

Russ stopped slouching and stood up taller.

"You can figure out how to film this in your sleep. This is child's play for someone of your talent," Sugar said, her tone one of a woman who would not be fucked with. "We're seriously screwed right now and I need everyone to only tell me solutions, not problems. That includes you, Jackson."

Jackson narrowed his eyes at the words *seriously screwed*. Well, they weren't in the best situation here, but *seriously screwed* seemed a bit of an overstatement. Since Sugar wasn't one for exaggeration, something had happened while he was sleeping that had escalated things. He wondered what.

"The problem is the speed. I need to be in front of them," Russ was saying.

"Solutions," Sugar snarled.

"We could slow them down," Jackson said, only half paying attention as he debated what had gone wrong—or he should say *more* wrong. Maybe Hank had told her they weren't coming tomorrow morning. Maybe their rescue had been delayed. That would stress her to the hilt.

"How?" Russ asked, his tone bordering on excited.

"Golf carts have governors on them that can slow them down. We can turn them on, but your cart could have regular speed if you wanted to be in front."

"We'll have to run it several times," Russ said, walking back and forth in the street, sizing things up. "This won't be ideal. Or maybe I could set some stationary cameras up at intervals…" He wandered off toward the ticket booths.

"What's wrong?" Jackson asked quietly.

Sugar gave him an annoyed glance. "Don't."

"Okay," he said, backing off because the one word was filled with stress that bordered on panic.

"I mean it."

He patted the air. "Message received."

"Do *not* tell me to calm down."

He clutched his chest dramatically. "I would never."

"You just did," she said through clenched teeth. "With that calm down gesture."

"I see. I apologize completely."

She narrowed her eyes. "Don't placate me."

Russ came hurrying back. "Okay here is what we'll do." He pointed to the ticket sales area, which was covered by a roof with small booths inside, iron railings separating each of the six-foot-wide isles. "We start them inside under the roof so they burst out of the building. We have one cameraman stationed right outside to capture them coming out." He turned and pointed to the nearby corner. "We have another cameraman on that corner." He pointed down the street. "And I'll be at the finish line capturing the winner."

"Great plan, except we don't have two extra cameramen," Sugar said with a growl.

Whatever was wrong, she wasn't going to be charmed or comforted into a better mood. Hank must have told her he wasn't coming tomorrow at all. Or maybe the day after that, as mad as she was.

"Yes, we do." Russ grinned. "We have you and Cindy."

"Cindy is injured."

"I'm not asking her to run beside them. I'm asking her to hold a camera," Russ huffed. "You asked for solutions, Sugar."

Sugar closed her eyes and shook her head. "I did. You're right. Okay, Cindy and I will be cameramen. I was just hoping to be more involved in managing the scene, but we have to do what we have to do."

"I could hold a camera," Jackson said, wanting to take some of the burden from her.

"No, you'll be racing." Sugar studied the street as if it held a minefield.

"I will?" He had absolutely zero interest in racing. It occurred to him for the thousandth time that signing up to be the Bachelor had been a massive mistake. Not only did he not want to end up with one of these women, he also didn't like being the center of attention. He was a man who had been born to be in the background fixing things.

"Yes," Sugar said, and from her tone, she wasn't going to discuss it further. "Russ, take Jackson to help you bring up the golf carts."

"I have to start rigging the cameras."

She frowned. "I thought we were using people to hold them?"

Russ shook his head before she finished the sentence. "We'll need stationary cameras at ten-foot intervals to really capture this thing."

Sugar stared up at the heavens as if she were asking for help from a higher power. "Okay. Jackson would you help *me* bring up the golf carts."

Jackson couldn't stop the smile that spread across his lips, even though he knew it would annoy her. "I'd love to."

She frowned at him, then turned on her heel and marched to the golf cart. "I'll drive so you can drive up each of the five carts."

He climbed in beside her. "You don't want to use these two?"

"I think we should keep these to the side, in case of an emergency." She drove them at top speed to the warehouse.

"With the governors on, the likelihood of a wreck is almost nothing."

"At this point, we can't take chances," she said, her voice grim.

"What's happened?" he asked again. "You can trust me, Sugar. I can keep a secret." He didn't mean to remind her of what happened between them, but really, he thought it was pretty clear by now that he wasn't a man who let the cat out of the bag.

"I know." She blew out a breath. "I've been told not to tell you."

"Hank isn't coming tomorrow?"

She laughed, but not like it was funny. "Oh, Hank's coming. He swears he'll be here by eleven in the morning."

That brought Jackson up short. So, what was the problem? "Then why do you look like we've been given a death sentence?"

She pulled to a stop outside the warehouse. "Are you telling me I have that bad of a poker face? I really should find a new job."

If Sugar was thinking about quitting, things were way worse than he'd thought. "Sugar, just tell me what the problem is. I can't help if I don't know."

"Hank was adamant that even Russ couldn't know."

"If you don't bring me into the loop, you'll be without backup. I don't know what's wrong, but if you're this worried, backup will come in handy."

Sugar stared at the Admin Building, a look of defeat growing on her face. "This job is totally fucked and I don't think I can fix it."

"I will do everything in my power to help you be successful." He meant it. He was going to help her even though they couldn't be together. Even if it meant he had to be the Bachelor and embarrass himself for the rest of his life and choose to date a woman he had no interest in when all he wanted was the woman beside him. This woman, who he couldn't have.

She shook her head. "I have no idea why I trust you, but I do. I must be losing my mind." She tucked one leg up on the bench to face him. "Niles is not an Atlantis employee."

Whatever he'd come up with as the issue, he was totally blindsided by this news. "Uhhhh."

"That's what I said." She threw up her hands. "They can't seem to contact any of the employees and there is nothing Hank can do to speed up our rescue. He'll be here tomorrow with the park manager and his staff so they can get to the bottom of what's going on. But until then, we're on our own."

"You think Niles is behind all our bad luck?"

"He's like a million years old. Do you think he'd be able to build trapdoors like that? He can barely walk. Maybe we fell in by accident and it's just some sort of coincidence? I spent all night last night lying there thinking about the fact that if someone wanted to kill us, they could have easily done it. He'd just have to wait until we fell down into the tunnels then shoot us or something."

"The elevator could have killed us." Nothing made any sense. Why would someone want to impersonate a staff member of an amusement park? Sure, maybe a terrorist would do it, but not if the park was empty.

"Yeah, and I thought of that too. That's been the truly dangerous part in all this. But after that, it was the two trap doors and locking us in a circle in the tunnels."

"That room you fell into yesterday seemed more like a prison." And she'd still be down there if he hadn't gone looking for her. Sure, he'd fallen in himself, but he didn't think that was anyone's master plan. It was more like a bonus, if he hadn't gotten them out.

"Well, no matter what is happening, Hank wants us sticking by the apartments from now on. No more exploring the park. And we have to always have a buddy with us. I need to keep anyone from realizing what's going on, which means we use this race as a distraction."

He took the hint and got out of the cart. "If you want a distraction, you'll get a distraction," he said, buckling down to work. As he moved golf carts, he thought about how close she'd come to being trapped where no one would have known how to find her. He didn't like that at all. Sugar needed a buddy more than the rest of them, because once she was trapped, the others wouldn't be able to function without her leadership.

He was just going to have to be her shadow, even if that was the last thing she wanted.

Sugar wished she'd slept last night. By ten-thirty AM, she was seriously dragging ass. The contestants and a miserable looking Jackson were lined up in their golf carts under the tin roof of the ticket booth. She could tell he didn't like being the prize in this race. Well, they were all doing things they didn't like, so he could lump it.

"Okay!" she shouted over Jillian, who was laughing as she revved her engine. "Jillian, please."

The others snickered and Jillian quit revving.

Cindy would film the start area. Jackson had rigged up a wheelchair with an extension that held her leg up at the perfect angle. She'd been giddy at the prospect of getting out and participating. Sugar felt terrible that she hadn't given the older woman any attention, but she was only one person with way too many responsibilities. She had to give herself some grace.

"Here are the rules. The first person to reach the finish line," she pointed way down the street where they'd run a yellow streamer across the road, "wins a date with the Bachelor."

The women cheered.

"What happens if the Bachelor wins?" Lena asked.

"Ah!" Sugar raised one finger, knowing she had everyone's attention. This felt like a normal shoot. Everything organized and well thought out, going off without a hitch. "Then the Bachelor gets to choose his date."

Jackson's face flashed a look of horror before it went blank.

Well, he had signed up for this, what did he expect?

A sudden realization hit her like a thunderbolt. What if Jackson hadn't ever watched the show? He had no idea what was in store for him.

No. Surely he wasn't that stupid?

A small, petty piece of her wanted him to reject all these beautiful women and choose her. *Not going to happen. He's here to choose a fiancée. You will never be his choice for that.*

Her last long-term boyfriend had resisted a bigger commitment. Then, after she dumped him, he was engaged to someone three months later. *Always the bridesmaid, never the bride.* She'd long ago put all that behind her, so why was she wasting her time thinking about it when she needed to concentrate on filming?

The thought depressed her so much, she wanted to crawl in bed and sleep for a week. Instead, she would do her job to the best of her ability. She might have a fucked-up love life, but she wasn't going to ruin her professional life as well.

"I've got to go down to my filming spot on the corner, so Jackson will call the start after I give him the thumbs up." She gave Jackson two thumbs up to demonstrate, using her *let's-get-excited* face.

He frowned at her.

As she walked to her place, her heart lightened a bit. It wasn't as if Jackson was any happier about this than she was. She picked up her camera, turned it on, set it on her shoulder and held her thumb up above her head.

"On your mark," Jackson yelled.

Electric engines revved.

"Get set."

"Go!"

Mayhem broke out immediately when Raven came out of her chute at an angle, slapping into the iron railing, over-correcting, then slamming into Lena, whose golf cart skidded into a circle. Lena let fly a stream of curses Sugar could hear all the way down on the corner.

Sugar resisted the urge to zoom into the wreck, knowing that her job was to film the whole scene and Russ would splice together what he wanted.

Raven left Lena in the dust, putting the peddle to the metal to catch up to everyone.

"You bitch," Lena screamed after her.

Meanwhile, the other three had jumped forward at the speed of a snail, the governors keeping them to a crawl, but they were all neck and neck on the right side of the street, with Jackson's face screwed down in concentration. He obviously wanted to win. Following the action, Sugar idly wondered what he wanted so badly as his prize.

Jillian pulled ahead, nudging in front of Andi, then veering to the right to cut off the competition.

Andi jamming on the breaks to avoid a crash. "Cheater," she screamed. From her snarl of anger, Jillian hadn't heard the last of Andi's displeasure.

Sugar realized she'd zoomed in on Andi's face and missed the end of the race, but she recorded Andi's wrath as Jillian began to celebrate her victory at the finish line with hardy whoops. She wouldn't have thought sweet Andi could transform into a woman with thinned lips and narrowed eyes, shooting laser beams of hate down the road at her rival.

Sugar shivered as it hit her how very serious these women were about this competition. They didn't even know Jackson beyond what they'd seen of him on the last season of the Bachelor when he'd had a few cameos, but they wanted him badly.

The camera hung limply in her hand, still recording the sidewalk when Sugar walked to the finish. How had things gotten so crazy so quickly? It's like this place was full of bad juju.

She stopped when Jillian launched into Jackson arms, swinging them both around as Jackson kept her from falling.

"I won!" Jillian declared and kissed him, missing his mouth by millimeters.

The same mouth Sugar had enjoyed running up and down her naked body yesterday.

Jealousy crawled up Sugar's spine and left her hands shaking with the need to rip Jillian off him. She took a deep breath and blew it out trying to get ahold of a temper she didn't even know she had. What had she expected him to do? Let Jillian fall? Push the other woman dramatically away? He was way too nice of a guy for that. Besides, that's what he was here for—to find someone who wasn't her.

"Everything okay?" Cindy had rolled down the sidewalk while Sugar stood there battling jealousy for a man she could never have.

"Honestly, no." Sugar turned to face her so she couldn't watch what Jackson was doing. "This whole thing has been a disaster."

"Yeah, it has. I have to say, when Russ said Hank had approved this group date, I was flabbergasted. He's never let them meet prior to the first cocktail before. It's Hank's number one rule."

Sugar couldn't bring herself to confess to Cindy that Hank hadn't approved this. "Well, this season has gone FUBAR from the start and I was desperate for something to distract the contestants."

"They have been angrier than usual. This will certainly stir things up and start some fights." Cindy studied the body language of the others, nodding at the impending situation.

"Speaking of," Sugar said, seeing Lena marching over to Raven and Andi striding over to Jillian.

Russ had seen it too, and slunk into position to capture it all.

Sugar handed her camera to Cindy, who dutifully started filming.

"Everyone gather around!" she called to distract the coming storms.

The cast turned to her, their emotions fading, but Sugar knew it would only be a temporary delay. "Jillian, go get ready for your date," she said, taking Jillian safely out of the fray. There would be plenty of time to have drama later but right now, she needed to keep everyone on schedule. "The rest of you need to hop in your golf carts and follow me," she said, figuring she'd put them to work to keep them out of trouble.

"Sugar," Cindy murmured. Sugar leaned over so the other woman could whisper, "What date are Jackson and

Jillian going on?"

"I have no idea," she whispered back. "Can you figure something out? I'm so tired, my brain is misfiring."

Cindy tried to cover her surprise. "I'll think of something. You should try to fit in a nap today. A Wrangler needs to stay sharp."

"They need supervision."

"Leave the losers with me when you're done cleaning this up. I'll have them play games or something in the living room."

Sugar sighed in relief. She should have been leveraging Cindy more during all of this. She wasn't even sure why she hadn't been. Cindy was a pro. "You're a life saver."

"I am," Cindy said with a grin.

Sugar returned her attention to the women to find Russ filming Lena and Raven in a low volume insult fest.

"It's not like I meant to hit you," Raven said huffily, getting into her cart.

Lena had her hands on her hips. "Well, you *did*."

"Idiot."

"Bitch."

"Okay, let's head out. Follow me," Sugar said, jumping in her golf cart.

Andi maneuvered around the fighting women and promptly ran into the back of Sugar's golf cart. "Sorry," she said.

"Raven you come next," Sugar said.

"She doesn't deserve to be next," Lena said, jumping in her cart to cut Raven off.

Sugar pretended not to see them and started down the road, promptly leaving them all in the dust since her golf cart didn't have a governor on it. She stopped to let them catch up as they jockeyed for position.

Today was going to be the longest day of her life.

CHAPTER TWELVE

*R*uss came to stand beside him as they watched the women inching away at the pace of a brisk walk. "Well that will create drama for days."

"You sound like that's a good thing," Jackson said, as he realized he and Russ had somehow become friends over the last day. Sure, the other man was his exact opposite in a lot of ways, but at Russ' core was a man who loved wiring and camera set up and being a professional when it mattered. Those were all things Jackson respected.

"It is. Ratings rely on drama and to have drama, you need to create drama. None of them are going to forgive Jillian for cheating any time soon."

Cindy rolled up to them, looking a million times happier to be out of her room. "Sugar needs our help coming up with a date activity."

Jackson frowned at the thought of being forced to enjoy Jillian's company. He liked her, actually, and respected how well she'd handled herself after the elevator crash, he just didn't like feeling trapped. And, if he was honest, she wasn't Sugar.

"Sugar said she didn't want anyone going in a new building after she fell through another trapdoor yesterday. Good thing you were there to fish her out," Russ said, giving Jackson a grin.

"What about making some sort of food?" Cindy

suggested.

"I'm a terrible cook," Jackson lied.

"Dance lessons?"

"Please, for the love of God, no." The thought of an intimate tango with Jillian had him slightly nauseous. He always felt like Jillian was two steps away from eating him alive.

"Too bad we can't turn on the Ferris Wheel," Russ put in, staring down the street at the item in question, still impressive even though it wasn't lit up and spinning.

"No rides without a ride operator and the employees here seem to be MIA." Cindy hummed as she thought. "The submarine ride that shows all the local fishes would have been awesome."

Jackson sighed, reluctant to bring up his idea, but figuring if it helped Sugar, he should do it. "There is a kid's whale train down at the Catering Pavilion. Someone could drive us around the park in it."

"Great idea! I could attach cameras at different angles and I wouldn't have to be there." Russ' excitement was not contagious.

"Yeah," Jackson said.

Cindy gave him an appraising look. "You don't seem too happy about it." She was much too smart for Jackson's comfort.

"I wasn't exactly thrilled that she cheated, either," Jackson said, trying to cover his deteriorating mood at the fact that the only woman he liked was the one he couldn't have.

Cindy laughed at his pain, but not cruelly, more like she was enjoying the show. "I guess she screwed you out of a win, too. Who were you planning to take on your date?"

"I was going to take all of them," he said, figuring it didn't hurt to reveal his strategy. "It's too early to start singling any of them out."

"Smart," Cindy said with approval. "I like the whale train ride idea. Think you can get it running?"

"Yeah," he said, knowing that even if it needed

repairs, older engines were a piece of cake to fix. Jackson often thought going back to them would be a good thing, if the carbon emissions weren't so catastrophic on the environment.

Sugar came around the corner with all the women hanging off her golf cart.

"I'm going to go grab something quick to eat and be right back. Russ, you planning to come with me to get the train running?" Jackson wanted to disappear before he was cornered again.

"Yeah let me grab some cameras."

"I'll just sit here in the road," Cindy said pleasantly.

"Oh, I'm so sorry," Jackson said, feeling awful that he'd forgotten her. "Want me to carry you back upstairs?"

"I would rather not go back up yet. I think I'll drive the whale train on your date, if that's okay with you?" Cindy gave him an assessing look.

"That would work," Russ said, interjecting himself in the conversation, even though he'd already started walking away. "You have to watch Cindy, Jackson. She never misses a thing."

That was what Jackson was afraid of.

Sugar watched Cindy drive the whale train down the road, feeling lower than she'd ever felt before. Jillian and Jackson sat cuddled in the last car. Nausea at the sight curled through her insides. She really had no one else but herself to blame for being jealous. Once they'd taken their clothes off and had fooled around, there was a piece of Sugar that had claimed him as hers. Or maybe that had happened when she'd held his amazingly perfect cock in her mouth. Desire whipped through her at the memory of his scent, the smell of limes and cedarwood she could still detect in her hair when it had fallen into her face while she'd been filming.

She had to let him go.

She didn't want to.

Well, that's just too bad. He wasn't hers and he would never be hers. Besides, it was probably some weird turn-on for having someone who was off limits. If she thought about it logically, their life goals were completely at odds. He didn't even want to live on this planet. Talk about a conflict.

She turned a circle trying to figure out what to do next since she didn't have an immediate crisis to attend to for the first time since she arrived.

Two blocks away, Niles hurried along the sidewalk away from her.

"Stop!" she ordered.

Niles didn't even pause, disappearing into Mike's Magical Knick Knacks.

Sugar didn't think, just broke into a run. "Niles," she called. "Wait." She needed to catch the old man and ask him questions, like if he was sabotaging filming and, if he was, why.

Skidding to a stop before the store, she cautiously pushed the door open and yelled inside, "Niles!" Her heart pounded in her chest as she peeked her head inside, but everything was still and quiet. She debated a moment before she slid inside and stopped to listen again. A door slammed in the control room.

She scanned the aisles as she eased through the store, not taking for granted that Niles was the cause of the noise. That was how people died in the horror movies. Not that Niles was going to kill her. Even the trap door she'd fallen through had landed her on a mattress to break her fall.

Slipping past the counter, she glanced quickly into the control room, then rolled back out of sight, like she'd seen cops do on reality TV when she'd been researching other shows with open positions. She clutched her clipboard tightly to her chest, wondering if it would do any damage if she had to fight Niles off with it. Maybe she should look for a better weapon.

No time. If she stayed out here too long, Niles would simply come back and jump her. The time to confront him was now.

The quick look had revealed only a black hole, so she slipped her hand along the wall until she flipped on the light, keeping her body in the magic shop in case Niles was in the control room.

Her next glance showed the room was empty.

A door on the far side stood open, the padlock dangling from where someone, she assumed Niles, had left it on the hook.

She debated the wisdom of going further. Niles knew the tunnels so much better than she did. In fact, she would grade herself as an F in that department, unlike Jackson, who had figured out the tunnel system in a snap.

Jackson was currently off canoodling with Jillian in the whale train.

That wasn't a vision she needed distracting her right now, so she shoved it away to concentrate on her current predicament.

Only an idiot would race after a madman, but she would really like to ask Niles some questions.

Well, too bad, Sugar thought as she suppressed the urge to follow, crossing the room in four quick strides. She was learning to deal with disappointment on so many levels.

She closed the door and put the padlock on through the clasp to block someone from returning to the control room. There. Now he was locked someplace he didn't want to be. Let him try that on for size. Although since he knew the tunnels so well, Niles could just exit somewhere else. Still, he'd be inconvenienced and that gave her at least some semblance of revenge.

She crumpled in the chair she'd been sitting in when she'd last spoke with Hank, cradling her clipboard tightly to her chest. This job had turned into a disaster on every level.

She would be naïve to hope that the crash and burn wouldn't engulf her career.

Maybe she wasn't cut out for love shows. Sugar knew she was being maudlin, but really, her one big shot had turned into the opposite of a resume stuff.

It wasn't just the elevator, or the trap doors, or the endless tunnels. She'd ended up falling for the talent.

She might as well admit that. Lying to herself about that would be silly.

Jackson was a great guy. Sweet, smart, dependable. Good in bed.

She sighed. Well, that ship had sailed and despite the fact she'd gotten his clothes off, he was *not* hers. He was here to do a job, just like she was and he was being much more of a professional than she, going on this date with Jillian like he was contractually obligated to do.

He might be attracted to Jillian.

He might. In fact, he should be. That's what they were all here for.

"Oh, who am I kidding," Sugar growled out loud. "I hope he has a terrible time."

"Who are you talking to?" Russ asked from the doorway.

Sugar jumped, barely managing not to tumble off the chair. "Oh my god Russ, you scared me."

"Sorry," Russ said and genuinely looked it.

"I followed Niles in here," she said, to distract him.

"Yeah?" Russ looked around at the obviously bare room.

She pointed to the door. "I put the lock on to keep him out."

"You didn't go after him?"

"Do I look like an idiot?" she growled.

"Absolutely not," Russ said hastily. "I wonder if I have him on camera." Russ moved to the computer bank and tapped some keys.

"You can access your cameras from here?"

"Yeah it's easier than on my handheld." Russ brought the screens to life and pulled up his camera feeds with only a couple clicks. "I figured why not send my feed to these, since no one else was using them."

"Russ, you're a genius." Energized, she joined him at the console.

Within minutes, Russ had the appropriate footage called up and they watched Niles slinking down the street.

"Can you back up? Show where he came from?"

Russ rewound the film. "There," he pointed.

Sugar consulted the map on her clipboard, since the view of the shop name was obscured. "Last Minute Quick Shop, I think. Maybe he needed supplies."

"He wasn't carrying anything."

"Play it again."

Russ rewound and watched the footage of Niles leaving the shop, crossing the street, going down a block, and entering Mike's.

She studied her map. "No, not the Quick Shop. Barney's Menagerie."

"Let's go see what he was doing."

She tapped her clipboard with a finger, debating. "Hank said not to go into any new places."

"Aren't you curious?"

"Of course." She was torn. "What if he pops out and grabs us?"

"That makes no sense. If he had access to the tunnels from over there, why would he come to Mike's?"

"True." She really wanted to figure out what Niles was doing. She glanced at her watch. "The contestants will get restless if we leave them alone for too long."

"They need to stew about Jillian's cheating for a bit and get themselves all riled up." He brought up the cameras to show them sitting in a circle in the shared living room.

"You have a point," Sugar said, knowing that drama

would be incoming when Jillian and Jackson returned. "Let's go, but we have to be extra careful not to end up falling through any trap doors." If they fell again, they'd have only themselves to blame.

"We'll stay spaced out so one of us can rescue the other." Russ was out the door before he finished talking.

They hustled down to the Barney's, the handle turning easily when they tried it. Then they both stood back so the other could enter.

"You go first," Sugar said, waving a hand.

"As the cameraman, I think we both know I'm more important."

"Than the Head Wrangler? I don't think so," Sugar said, miffed. Officially, they were at the same level of crew status, although she knew Russ was paid more since his job required more technical knowledge.

"Without me, the show literally can't go on," Russ said piously, taking another step backwards. "Plus, I can film you going in." He held up his camera.

Sugar snorted, but time was ticking so she stepped inside, getting out her flashlight to locate the light switch, which she found in a jiff. When the room flooded with light, they both stopped in surprise.

The shelves were filled with glass fish, whales, and sea creatures. The light reflected on their surfaces making the whole room sparkle.

"Whoa." Russ forgot that only one of them was supposed to be in the store at a time and wandered past her to touch a giant trout in the middle of the room on a round pedestal. "Who buys this shit?" he asked in wonder.

She had no idea. "Stay on target, Red Leader," she said, passing him to carefully study the floor as she made her way to the cash register area. "We're looking for why Niles was in here. It had to be something important for him to risk being seen by us." She cautiously worked her way around the cashier desk, but no trap door or hidden exit revealed itself.

"This fish has a name," Russ said with a snicker.

"Russ," Sugar said, infusing annoyance in the word.

"All right, all right, I'm looking." He moved deeper into the store while Sugar rifled through all the drawers of the register for anything that screamed *clue*.

"This is just regular business stuff." She studied the room, which was filled with nothing but shelf after shelf of inventory. "Do you see what he could have been in here for?"

"Nope. There isn't even a place for a hidden door here. All the walls are covered in shelving."

"He has to have come in here for a reason," Sugar said, irritated. What was Niles up to?

Another ten minutes of searching revealed nothing.

"We're wasting our time," she said, giving the room one last, hopeful sweep, before returning in defeat to International Street.

"Bye, Harold," Russ said over his shoulder as he pulled the door shut.

Sugar froze. "Harold who?" she asked, an echo of what she'd said yesterday when she spoke to Niles.

"That's the name of the trout."

Sugar couldn't believe it. She reversed course and went back inside, grabbing the place card to read, *Harold the Trout, King of the Lake*.

"What's wrong?"

"Niles was watching a fish named Harold."

"When?"

"Yesterday. He was sitting on a bench behind the apartments."

They both stood there, as confused as they'd been when they'd first come in.

"You think he was visiting this glass sculpture?" Doubt filled Russ' words.

"Yeah, that would be stupid. But naming a fish and waiting for him every day is kind of crazy, too."

"Yeah," Russ agreed. "If he's got some weird thing

for this statue, then maybe he'll come back. I'll put a camera facing the shop and have it send out a ping if he returns."

"With the cell tower down, can you do that?"

"Yep."

"How?"

Russ shrugged one shoulder. "I have my ways." He left the store. "I'm heading back to my room to grab some equipment."

Sugar stepped outside, just in time for the whale train to round the corner down the street. Part of her wanted to hide, but she was Head Wrangler. Even if it sucked, she had a job to do. She stepped to the curb and slapped on a smile as she waited for them.

CHAPTER THIRTEEN

𝒥ackson tried to enjoy Jillian's company, but he was having trouble with all her constant touching. For the first time in his life, he understood exactly how women felt when they were groped by unwanted hands at a bar.

When Jillian had made a dive down his pants, he'd caught her hand and said, "Whoa now, you've just met me. That's strictly off limits."

Jillian had laughed as if he'd made a great joke, but his patience had rapidly gone downhill from there. When Cindy had turned them around at the end of the park to go home, he had breathed a sigh of relief that the ride was half over. By the time they'd made it onto International Street, Jackson had reached a painful conclusion that he just couldn't fake this. He had to call Hank Carson and resign. Even knowing he'd never have Sugar, he still couldn't help the fact his heart had chosen her and wouldn't be swayed by anyone else, no matter how beautiful or smart or witty they were. It wasn't fair for him to pretend—not for him and certainly not for the contestants.

His dreams of going back up into space were over.

That depressed him, but still he helped Jillian out of the train and hugged her back when she hugged him, relief making him almost giddy at the thought of never seeing her again.

"Welcome back," Sugar said brightly. She'd obviously

moved on, their time together not impacting her as it had him.

Well, good for her. It was annoying, but that was the way the ball bounced when it came to affairs of the heart. Sometimes you were the windshield, sometimes you were the bug.

"Jackson, that was so much fun," Jillian cooed.

It hadn't been, but he smiled and said, "Thanks for coming with me."

Russ had magically materialized by his side to film their return with a handheld camera. Jackson dug deep and ignored him.

"I wouldn't have missed it for the world." She gazed soulfully into his eyes, her own big blue orbs shining with the possibility of love. She rose onto her tiptoes.

Jackson resisted the urge to grab her by the shoulder to hold her lips away from his own, but couldn't stop his frown.

"Date's over Jillian," Cindy called to them, saving him from having to give Jillian the forearm shiver.

"Awww," Jillian said, pouting. "Next time," she told him like a promise.

"Bye," Jackson said, hoping the word didn't convey his excitement to be rid of her.

Jillian drifted toward the women's apartments, an extra shake in her hips possibly caused by the high heels that made her rival Jackson's own height.

"How was the date?" Sugar asked.

A monstrous annoyance built in him that she sounded so peppy when he'd been all but soul-sucked by Jillian the Dementor. "I have to call Hank," he said and struck off down the road.

"What happened?" Sugar asked Cindy behind him.

"It was a long whale ride," Cindy said, her tone filled with amusement.

Jackson's annoyance ratcheted up a notch at Cindy's snicker. He picked up speed as he crossed the street.

"Wait, Jackson," Sugar said, her sneakers slapping on the pavement as she raced to catch up. She'd switched to tennis shoes he'd noticed. The boots might give her height and look sexy, but Atlantis had made her rethink her footwear. "Where are you going?"

He stopped and pivoted to face her. "Sugar, I know your job is important to you and I understand your desire to stop what is between us so it won't impact your career success. I respect that." The words were stiff, but really, what the hell was he supposed to say? "However, I have to do what I think is right and I would appreciate it if you could give me the space I need just as I'm giving you space."

Sugar looked hurt. "I'm sorry if you think I'm meddling, but it is my job."

Jackson hardened his heart. "I mean this with the utmost respect, but go do your job somewhere else." He wasn't going to beg Sugar to have feelings for him, or beg her to quit her job. She had the right to do what she needed to do in her life. Just because he thought they had something special didn't mean she had to throw everything she'd worked so hard for away for him. He didn't even want her to do that. Well, he did, but he wished he didn't.

"Hey Sugar," Cindy called from the train. "Can you give me a lift from the Catering Pavilion after I put the train up?"

Sugar ignored her. "If you have a complaint about me, I would prefer to hear it from you before you tell Hank, so I have a chance to work through your concerns."

Jackson huffed out a laugh. "I really don't think you want to hear what I have to say. And it isn't about you, anyway. It's about me." He held up a hand to stop her when she opened her mouth to argue. "Thank you for your concern, but what I have to say is something I need to speak with Hank about."

"Sugar, I need help," Cindy yelled from the whale.

"Jackson," Sugar said, and something on her face

made him pause, her look holding a combination of regret and need. Then the expression faded. "Never mind." She turned to help Cindy.

Jackson suppressed the sudden urge to sweep her up in his arms and carry her away. Since the reason she'd rejected him was that her job was more important, he turned on his heel and stalked to Mike's Magical Knick Knacks.

Hank answered on the second ring. "Carson."

The one word was filled with such annoyance, Jackson almost hung up the phone and tried again later. But putting this off wouldn't do anyone any good.

"This is Jackson Wright."

"Has something gone wrong?" Hank asked, his voice filled with so much concern, Jackson would have been suspicious even if he hadn't known what was truly happening down here.

"I'm calling to resign as the Bachelor."

"You can't resign," Hank said, switching from concern to annoyance in a flash.

"I can and I am. I didn't sign up for all this." He paused, figuring Hank deserved to know the truth. "And frankly Hank, I'm not cut out for this role."

Hank sighed. "I was worried about that, but I thought I could limp you through it. I knew things were in trouble when I couldn't get down there to bolster you mentally."

That took Jackson completely by surprise, especially since he didn't think he needed to be bolstered. However, Hank's honesty made him even more honest in return. "I didn't realize how much I hate being the center of attention. And I can't stand the women climbing all over me."

"Climbing? What do you mean climbing? You shouldn't have been interacting with them at all."

Jackson realized his mistake immediately. "Hank, after the elevator collapse and Cindy was hurt, Sugar was left dealing with us on her own, especially when Russ disappeared for so long. There was no way to totally keep us separate. You know there wasn't."

"Well, Sugar should have tried." Hank's ire was clear through the phone lines.

Jackson raced to smooth over the damage he'd inadvertently done to Sugar's job. "She did. Sugar has worked her ass off for you and anything that went wrong is not her fault. But this is a total cluster fuck down here and those women are a complete handful."

"Being Head Wrangler—"

"Sugar is the best, but this went beyond anyone's capability. Something is happening here," Jackson said, careful not to let Hank know he knew about Niles. "I don't know what, but things aren't right. The elevator, the trapdoors, getting locked down in the tunnels because doors shut and locked behind us."

"What doors were locked?"

Jackson wondered why Sugar hadn't told Hank. This conversation had gone completely down the drain. Sugar was going to hate him for it. "When Russ was missing, we were looking for him and somehow the doors locked us down there for a while. We made it out okay, but this isn't a normal place, Hank. It's dangerous."

"Why were you even with Sugar?"

"Because Russ was lost and Cindy's leg means she's stuck in bed. Someone had to help her search. She'd sent the women to the apartments. There was no chance of cross contamination." That's what Jackson felt like—like a virus to be contained.

"I'll be there in—" A pause while Hank did the math. "Seventeen hours. Just hold on until then."

"I'm going to make sure we hold on, but I'm giving you advance warning that you'll have my resignation in writing when you arrive."

"We'll talk about this when I get there. You need this money, Jackson."

"Yeah I do," Jackson said, for the first time in his life

feeling like he was a failure. "But I'll have to make it another way. I'm not going to find love here, Hank, and I can't fake it. I just hope you can bring in someone else to replace me, because I'm going home the minute you get us out of here." Jackson wanted to dramatically say something like *If I can't have Sugar, I don't want someone else.* But to protect her job, he didn't have that luxury.

Hank was silent on the other end of the phone.

"See you in seventeen hours Hank," Jackson said, and gently replaced the receiver.

He was free, but instead of feeling euphoric, Jackson just felt tired.

⌒

Sugar had made sure the contestants had been fed, trying to keep them civil until everyone had eaten something, but the fighting had already begun before she'd called them into the kitchenette for dinner. Never having the time to learn to cook, she'd made her home standby of pasta and red sauce, wishing she had some protein to put in it that might have helped even out some of the tempers.

Then, breaking a long-standing rule, she ate with the cast so she could give them a bit of a break from the war she knew had broken out between them. They were naturally on their best behavior around her, but Lena wasn't speaking to Raven and no one was speaking to Jillian.

"What happens tomorrow?" Andi asked, filling the silence.

"Hank Carson should be here around eleven and we'll probably have an all-cast meeting with him to find out the new plan." Sugar hoped Hank had a plan, because she was all out of ideas. In fact, when this was over, she knew that she would be blamed for how badly things had gone, even though it wasn't really fair. It hadn't been her fault that the elevator had a catastrophic failure. It wasn't her fault Cindy was hurt or Russ fell through a trapdoor. But the job of the Head

Wrangler was to work with the impossible and make everything come out roses in the end. There was the slightest chance things could still work out, but her hopes were rapidly dying.

Further complicating matters, as she watched Jillian hugging Jackson, Sugar had realized that her time as a Wrangler on a love show was over. She needed a change. When she got home, she'd update her resume and get the word out she was looking for work.

"The point is," Lena said out of the blue, "you sabotaged me by running into my cart."

"Not on purpose," Raven said around a mouth full of spaghetti. "It didn't matter anyway, because Jillian would have gotten you in the end."

All the women stared daggers at the blond woman.

"Yeah, like she did me and Jackson," Andi snarled.

"Jackson was more than happy with the outcome, I can assure you," Jillian said self-righteously.

"Sure he was. We saw him from the window and he looked like he was going to run from you."

Sugar agreed Jackson hadn't appeared happy at the end of the ride, but he didn't seem upset either.

"You know," Jillian said, frustration in her tone. "This is a game. We're supposed to try our hardest to win so we can spend time with the man of our dreams."

"You're supposed to not cheat," Raven declared.

"Funny *you* of all people should say that," Lena sniffed.

Sugar rested her head in her hands. This was doomed. She couldn't salvage it. She'd let the cast get too far out of control too early in the process and Hank would tell her rightly that it was all her fault.

"Are you okay, Sugar?" Andi asked, concern in her voice.

"This is all my fault. I should have never let you guys race. It's poisoned your relationships." They'd been perfectly fine yesterday, all so focused on hating the circumstances of the game that they had grown closer because of it.

Sugar realized she needed help and she needed it now. While she was tempted to call Lynette, there was no way someone on the surface could understand exactly what was happening down here.

She stood, leaving her food unfinished on the table and went to find Cindy.

"Good chat," Raven called after her, exasperated.

"What's gotten into her?" Jillian asked.

"It's shocking you of all people are asking, since you only care about yourself," said Lena.

"Ooooh! Burn," Raven said with glee.

This is my fault. Sugar picked up speed, down the stairs, across the street, back up the other stairs and down the crew apartments hall, but Cindy wasn't in her room.

Sugar stood there debating where she could be. Someone with as bad of an injury as she had couldn't have gotten far. After an internal debate where she considered asking Jackson, she went in search of Russ instead to see if he knew where Cindy was.

On the way to Russ' room, Jackson's closed door called to her, but she left without knocking.

She found Russ on her second try in the back office behind Mike's. He was reviewing film of the Great Clusterfuck, which is what she was calling the golf cart race in her mind. "Oh God," she said, seeing Lena's snarl.

"This is gold," Russ said, his voice triumphant. "Hank is going to love it."

"No, he isn't. He's going to flip out."

"Why would he—" Russ' hands stilled. "Tell me you didn't do this behind his back?"

"Okay, I won't tell you." She flopped into the chair that was starting to feel like her own.

"Sugar," he said.

"I know." She didn't need a speech repeating the

things she's told herself already. "They were talking about quitting. I was desperate to keep them happy."

Russ shook his head. "You ended up with great film," he said, trying to look on the bright side for her.

"Yeah." She stared at Andi's outraged face. "They hate each other now. It's too early for that."

"You can salvage it."

"Can I?"

"Maybe," Russ conceded. "It will take a little luck, but when Hank gets down here, he can pull it off. He's the master of luck."

Across the room on the far console, a muted beeping began. The screen above it helpfully flashed the word *Warning!* in red.

She and Russ froze.

The beeping continued.

Sugar approached the console as she would a snake, Russ slightly behind her. "What's an air terminal A123?" she asked, reading the small print on the screen.

"No clue."

They both stood there for a moment. As the Head Wrangler, it was her job to do something, she just wasn't sure what.

The warning beep continued without resolving itself.

This is what she got for trying to avoid Jackson. The universe was pulling them together.

She pivoted to the door.

"Where are you going?"

"To get Jackson." If anyone would know what was happening, he would.

Wasn't that what an engineer did? Fix stuff like this? She had no idea.

As she ran to the crew apartments, she remembered that she had originally been looking for Cindy. Well, shit. First thing's first. She needed to have someone figure out what the scary beeping was about. Then she'd find Cindy.

CHAPTER FOURTEEN

Jackson figured he'd work some anxiety off by doing pushups. He'd gotten through half of the pushup pyramid, which would end at one hundred, when someone banged on the door.

"Enter," he said, but kept going. The pushup pyramid was hard but stopping only drew out the pain. Better to finish than to take a break. His arms screamed and his abs quivered, but he was almost there.

Sugar came into the room and froze. "Why do you have your shirt off?" she asked in a strangled voice.

"Working out." He knew he was being short, but really it was hard to maintain civility when things were this messed up. Howling at the moon and throwing a fit were not an option, more's the pity. Instead he'd just have to try to be polite until he escaped as far from Sugar as he could get. She wanted him to back off, so he would. He'd back off to Siberia if he had to, which he might since being on the same planet with Sugar wouldn't stop him from wanting her.

Open mouthed, she stood there watching his body for a long second and part of him enjoyed it. *This is what you're missing*, he wanted to tell her. *This could be all yours.*

He knew he wasn't being fair, but he was still working through the stages of grieving. They would have been perfect for each other. She had to know that.

She doesn't want to live in space. Well, there was that.

Everything else was perfect. Chemistry like theirs didn't come along every day. He knew that for a fact. A relationship like theirs would take some sacrifice but would ultimately be worth it.

Sugar took a big breath. "Focus," she said, most likely to herself since she was certainly focused on him. "We have an alarm going off in the office behind Mike's."

Seventy-one. He kept going. He had just completed the hardest part in the middle. After about seventy, things shifted and became super easy, the end in sight. He figured that would be how it was after he left the show and Sugar. If he could get past a certain point, all this awful longing and need would fade and he would be on the downhill slide into healing. "What kind of alarm?"

"Air terminal A123. That's all it says besides Warning!"

Intrigued despite himself, he dropped a knee to the floor. "Niles said something about air handler issues," he said, remembering back to their weird meeting on the street.

"When did you speak with Niles?"

"Russ and I saw him when we went down to get the radios and pick up more camera equipment." He'd have to finish later. To know what the issue was, he'd have to go to Mike's. He stood up and toweled off quickly.

Sugar's eyes followed the towel, her mouth held in a small O.

It saddened him to end the moment, but he threw on a shirt and yanked himself into the here and now. "Let's go take a look." Because a system failure with an air handler would be a bad thing. Not good at all. He needed to concentrate and stop torturing Sugar. At least she still wanted him. That much was clear. Good, because he didn't feel like being the only person hurting here.

He led, moving so fast, she had to jog beside him, his mind distracted by what differences there might be between air systems in space verses under water. He figured there would be some similarities. At least the basics would be the same.

Russ was in the control room when they walked in. "Yo," he said, not looking away from the film he was reviewing.

"How long has this been going off?" he asked, because Russ wasn't acting appropriately concerned.

"Just started before Sugar went to find you."

Jackson touched and held his finger to the screen. The warning notice expanded.

"Wish I'd known the secret engineer handshake," Sugar said beside him.

He read through the list of reported issues, frowning when he wanted to smile. He was done being amused by Sugar's fantastic wit and quick mind. "Air handler 123. Russ, can you bring up a schematic of Atlantis for me and find where it's located? I'm going to need to take a look at the machine itself. Best case, it will need a hard reboot. Worst case, we'll need Hank to bring down parts." Actually, that wasn't exactly true. Worst case, they'd run out of air and die, but he didn't think saying that out loud would do anyone any good. Besides, a place like this had to have redundancies out the wazoo.

"Got it," Russ said. "Here, in a building called the Physical Plant." When Russ touched the map he'd pulled up on the screen, the whole area popped forward into more detail.

Jackson scanned the schematic. "There are only two air handlers here. I would have thought there would be more for this big of space." Not good. Not good at all. "Have either of you seen Niles?" After all, Niles said he'd been working on them. The best place to start would be with the person who knew what was happening.

"We saw him coming out of Barney's Menagerie when you were on your whale date," Sugar said.

"He was looking at a glass fish named Harold," Russ

said, snickering.

"We don't know that," Sugar said in a cadence that spoke of an earlier disagreement.

"You said when you saw him the first day, he was talking to a fish named Harold. Barney's had a fish sculpture named Harold. Besides, there was nothing else there that made sense."

Jackson shook his head, not sure what to do with the information that the man who knew what had gone wrong with the air handlers might be totally nuts. "Russ, call Hank and tell him we're having issues with the air handlers and ask what the emergency protocols are here." They had to have some. No way OSHA would let them run this place without backups on top of backups. This most likely sounded much worse than it was.

"Are you going to go look at it?" Sugar asked.

A nice guy would leave Sugar alone and let what they had between them fade away. He decided he wasn't a nice guy. "Both of us are. I need someone to hold the flashlight and hand me tools." He knew she didn't want to be alone with him, but she'd just have to suck it up. "Russ, I'm going to need you to talk me through where to go on the radio when I get into the building." He tapped the screen to pull up the building blueprint.

"Wait," Russ said, hustling from his chair to a backpack leaned against the wall. "I need to put a camera on each of you."

"Russ," Sugar growled. "We don't have time for this."

"We have to make time. You know as well as I do we have to film everything." Russ blocked the doorway as he rummaged through the pack.

"Quickly," Jackson said, not wanting to fight Russ' sudden backbone.

Russ pinned a camera to each of their right shoulders. They were a size of a fist and weighed almost nothing. "You never know when good film will happen."

Sugar huffed. "Right. You're just looking for blooper material."

"Blooper reel is only a side benefit," Russ said, sounding hurt. "The difference between an Emmy and a cancelled show is the nuanced moments only a great cinematographer can capture."

"Oh-kay," Jackson said. "We'll call you on the radio when we get there."

As Jackson walked out, he could hear Russ saying, "Hank, we have a problem," on the phone behind them. "Yeah, another one."

"I'm driving," he said, getting into the lead golf cart and peeling off the moment her butt hit the passenger side of the bench.

Sugar grabbed on, her body smashing into him when they rounded the corner. "Aren't we going the wrong direction?"

"We need to stop by the Catering Pavilion for some tools." He concentrated on pushing the cart to its maximum.

"What's your plan?"

"I'll know for sure when I get there, but most likely I'll try rebooting first. We only need it to last another fourteen hours. That might hold off any slow-evolving problem. If it's an acute issue, we might be in trouble."

"If I die down here, I'm coming back as a ghost to haunt Hank for the rest of his days," Sugar declared as he skidded to a stop.

He'd already composed a list of tools they needed, so they had them stuffed into a crew backpack within three minutes of arriving. He grabbed headsets for each of them so they'd have their hands free.

"Should we grab some rope in case one of us falls through another trapdoor?" Sugar asked, demonstrating that she was a woman after his own heart.

He found some on a peg and added it to the top of the pack. Then they were roaring up to International Street and onto Amusement Way. The maintenance shed was back behind the roller coaster on the far side of the park.

"When you saw Niles, what exactly did he say?"

He tried to remember what he and Russ had been talking about when they saw the strange man. "We were discussing Hank, actually. Russ said Hank wouldn't cancel the show, just because of the elevator."

"He wouldn't, but I think Hank knows his opportunity to salvage this shoot is rapidly draining away. I honestly don't know how he's going to save this. Even as good as he is, it will take a miracle."

Jackson figured even Hank Carson would know when he was defeated once he got down here and saw what a cluster it was. "I quit the show," he said, figuring she'd hear soon enough.

Her mouth dropped open. "You did?"

"Yeah." He took a corner a little too fast. The back wheels slid out behind them. He steered into the skid and righted them, but not before Sugar let out a cute little squeak.

"Slow it down there, cowboy," she said, breathless.

He laughed and realized he felt better than he had since he'd arrived in Atlantis. Except for the time when he had Sugar naked and at his mercy. He would relive that moment in his memories for the rest of his life.

"I can't believe you quit. What about the money?"

He stepped on the breaks, the cart shuttering to a stop. Turning, he put his arm along the back of the seat and met her gaze. "There is no money on this planet worth me faking interest in other women when the one I want is sitting on this seat beside me."

Her mouth formed an O, her eyes huge.

He grabbed the backpack of tools and circled the cart to the building.

Sugar scrambled out behind him.

He tried to ignore her. After all, he had an important job to do here, but just being with Sugar made him want to touch her.

Trying to get his head back where it belonged, he grabbed the door handle and pulled, only to have his hand snap back empty. "It's locked," he said, getting out his picks.

"That's weird. Niles has been leaving doors open all over the park."

"Yeah." His internal alarm trilled, warning him that the locked door meant something important, even if he didn't know what yet. But Niles had locked this door for a reason. Although hadn't Niles said something about guests not being allowed in the maintenance building? Maybe he'd simply locked it because of security protocols. Although, if he wasn't an employee, he wouldn't be following protocols...

Focus. Rushing only made his hands shake and the tumblers fall back into place. He took a deep breath and let it out, then gave the lock another try. Slow movement was the key to success. "There," he said, as it opened.

They walked inside, flipping on lights, saving energy costs long ago forgotten. The wall had a helpful sign that listed out the different sections of the building. Park Systems was straight ahead down a dark hall.

"Russ," he said on his radio.

"Here," Russ' voice came immediately. "I can see where you are. The camera has a tracker."

Jackson and Sugar exchanged a look. Sugar sighed in annoyance. "Well, it will help locate us if we end up falling into the tunnels again."

"Go straight along the hall and pass through the door to the left," Russ said helpfully.

Jackson clipped the radio to his belt and put on the headset so he could have his hands free.

They moved down the hall with one eye on the ground watching for telltale signs of trapdoors, then turned left to find a bare room except for a large rug that covered the middle of the floor. "Better go around," he said, catching Sugar's hand and steering her to the edge.

"The air handlers should be down the stairs in the next room," Russ' voice said.

Jackson sighed. Of course they were in the basement. It would be too easy to have it up here where it would be less creepy. He drew them both to a stop. "I'm getting a little sick of the basement in this place."

"Me too." She peered down the stairs into the darkness, then looked around. "No light switch." She pulled out her flashlight and ran the beam over the door at the bottom.

"You have to go down in the basement," Russ reminded them.

"At least we can't fall through a trapdoor if we're on the bottom level," Sugar pointed out.

"That's one of the things I love about you. You're a glass half full kind of gal."

"I try to be. Negativity stresses people out for no reason."

"Good point." One he agreed with. There was a moment he thought they might die on Genesis III, after Alphie had taken over. Then he realized that there was nothing left to do but eat a nice meal, figuring he'd make the best out of his last hours. He really did like to eat. That was something he missed badly when he was in space where the food ranged from inoffensive to just plain awful. Since he was going to stay on Earth for at least the time being, he could eat out every place that struck his fancy.

They took the stairs slowly, not rushing but not lollygagging either. When they opened the door at the bottom of the stairs, they heard a buzzer blaring from a bank of machines along the far wall.

Sugar veered to turn the lights on. One bulb in the center of the room lit up when she hit the switch.

"Here." Jackson hit the button to silence the alarm on the left of two identical machines, each as tall as he was and about three of him wide.

"What's the plan?"

"This air handler is only running at 20%. I think the first thing we should do is reboot the system. It could be it's some sort of simple fault that will be fixed in the boot stage."

"That doesn't sound like a good long-term strategy."

"Long term is the park's problem. *We* won't be here long term. We're going to be here until eleven AM when Hank is going to get me, at least, the hell out of here." If he was staying on Earth, he'd need to buy a house and maybe a car. For a moment, he was distracted by what would come next, then he pushed all those thoughts aside and scanned the gages of the right machine, comparing them to the left. Niles had been right. This place was fragile.

"Don't you think someone has tried rebooting by now?"

"Unless I've done it myself, I assume no one has taken basic steps. It's safer that way." Jackson located the on/off switch. "There is one other small concern."

"What's that?"

"Can the park can run on only one of these at a time?" The right air handler was running at 100%. With the park deserted, that should be enough, although what did he know? "I would assume it can since there is no way this place doesn't have redundancies."

"I feel like that's not enough to reassure me," she said, staring at his finger which rested on the off switch.

"On the bright side, there aren't a bunch of guests here and no rides are running that will gobble up the oxygen. Oxygen needs should be minimal."

"Valid point."

"Here goes nothing," he said and flipped the switch. A loud humming groaned and sputtered. Then silence filled the air and he understood for the first time just how much louder this air handler was from identical one standing beside it.

From somewhere to their left in the darkness, someone yelled, the words unintelligible.

Neither of them moved.

A moan echoed from the darkness.

"That's the sound I heard right before I ended up falling through a trapdoor," Sugar said.

"Eight, seven," he said, counting down from twenty.

She raised an eyebrow. "Your approach to fixing this system doesn't seem very sophisticated."

"Five, start simple. A horse is usually a horse, not a zebra."

"What?"

"Three, Two, One Blast off," he said, and flipped the switch.

The air handler started up and immediately paused. The small computer screen asked, *Start initiation sequence?*

From the darkness someone yelled again.

He pressed the "yes" option.

Starting initiation sequence.

Sugar stared into the dark doorway across the room. "Should we go find whoever is yelling?"

He figured they should, amazed at his lack of interest, but that's what Atlantis had done to him—made him question every decision as a potential lure that would end with them in an endless circle or falling down a slide into a mattress, trapped. Not that *that* misadventure hadn't been wonderful in the end. "I can't leave this until I'm sure it's made it through bootup."

"I'll go check alone then." Sugar squared her shoulders and peered into the darkness beyond the small circle of light in which they stood.

"You're not going alone. That's when a guy jumps out with a chainsaw," Jackson said, scanning a nearby desk for a manual for the air handler. If this restart didn't work, he'd need another plan. The warning in the control room wouldn't have sounded if they weren't in serious trouble

"There hasn't exactly been anyone jumping out at us, and certainly not with a chainsaw." There was a grin in Sugar's voice. "Although I'm finding myself reluctant to race off to save anyone."

He found the manual, pulling it from the nice, neat line of books stacked across the right side of the desk. "Here's what we're going to do. I'm going to stay right here, reading this manual while you go to the other side of the room and turn on the light in that next room to see what's there. Then when the initiation sequence has run its course, we'll go inside together."

"Sounds like a plan."

"Oh and Sugar?"

She turned and he stepped into her space. "A kiss for luck," he said and kissed her, just a quick press of his lips, following his instincts instead of his brain, which told him he was going to end up regretting pushing his luck.

Her lips hesitated and he almost pulled away, then she curled into him and tugged him closer.

Without her high heeled boots on, she was much shorter than him but electricity flew between them, the attraction still deep and right, even if they weren't going to be together. Forget about reality. He could stay here all night long and just love on Sugar.

A beep sounded and his brain flagged it as important. It still took him a long time to raise his head. He tried to remember what was happening. "Air handler," he said and stepped away.

"Right." She laughed, the sound a bit guilty. "And I'm going to check out the yelling sound without falling through a trapdoor."

"Sounds like a plan," he said, and grinned at her.

CHAPTER FIFTEEN

Sugar found a light switch and clicked it on. Instead of another room, the light revealed a short hallway with three doors, one on each side and the third at the end of the hall. All of the doors were open, the lights off.

"Muhhh!" someone said from down the hall to the left, this time quite clearly.

Unable to contain her curiosity, she inched down the hall and put her arm around the corner, sliding it along the wall to search for the switch as silently as possible. Finding it, she clicked it on, flooding the space with light.

Sugar peeked around the corner and found herself looking at a small, blond woman tied to a wheelchair, silver tape across her mouth. "Barbara?" Sugar asked, this time in a whisper.

Barbara, if it was Barbara, shook her head dramatically back and forth, her eyes wide looking... at something behind Sugar.

"Oh crap," Sugar said, as a large hand covered her mouth with a wet cloth.

Then everything went dark.

⌒

Jackson had gotten lost in the manual as the air handler slowly went through its boot up sequence. His mind launched into an assessment of how this air handler differed from the one they'd had on Genesis III. They were both based on the same technology, which was good. However, the more he read, the more he realized just how bastardized the one on the space station had been. It had been way too costly to fly up another, so the space engineers before him had made modifications, some of which had been more of the duct tape variety.

He suspected this air handler hadn't experienced the same amount of fiddling, although it was about the same age since Genesis III and Atlantis had been built around the same time. There were sections of the manual that had been high-lighted, which Jackson found odd. He read those sections twice, since someone had thought they were important.

The air handler beeped, signaling the end of the boot, dragging him from his thoughts.

He rose from the desk, instinctively looking for Sugar. Who wasn't there.

"Sugar?" he called, and a bad feeling crawled along his spine. She was right here last he knew. Or had she been? Had she come back from turning on the light down the hall?

Surely no one had grabbed her when he'd been sitting right here? He hadn't heard a thing. He was pretty sure the hyper-vigilante state he'd been operating in would have warned him.

A quick glance at the air handler showed it was running at 50%, so the reboot had worked, but there was still an underlying problem. Well, he'd have to worry about it after he found Sugar. Maybe she just wandered off while he'd been in his own world.

He stuck his head down the hall and called, "Sugar."

No response, not even the faint yelling they'd heard before.

He worked his way down the hall, looking into the two rooms with their doors open, both rooms empty. The third door at the end of the hall was closed. He tried the

160

handle and it opened beneath his hand. A tunnel greeted him.

He went back for his flashlight that was on the desk.

"Russ," he said into his radio.

Static answered him.

Of course the radios didn't work in the basement. Nothing here was that easy. He took the stairs back to the first floor and called again. "Russ?"

"Go ahead Jackson," Russ said in an official voice.

"Can you see Sugar's tracker?"

"Yeah. Why did you two split up?"

This wasn't the time for chit chat. "Can you see her feed?"

Pause, then, "It's dark but her video is still transmitting."

"Where is she?"

"The tunnels I think, since she's moving in a direct line with them."

Jackson was surprised Russ hadn't seen that they'd separated sooner. He'd probably gotten distracted by reviewing past footage. "I had to come back up to the first floor to reach you on the radio."

"We're having a drama here. Sugar needs to come back to Mike's as soon as possible," Russ said, explaining his lack of diligence.

"Sugar has disappeared."

"What do you mean, disappeared?"

"I mean, one minute she was with me, then she wasn't." That wasn't exactly true, but Jackson didn't have time to explain it all. If Russ could see Sugar's location, he'd take the golf cart and head her off from above. He ran up the stairs and through the room, forgetting about the rug until it started to collapse beneath him.

Launching his body forward, he landed half onto the floor, his legs swinging into the void below him. "Dammit," he said.

"What's happened?" Russ yelled from the headset,

which had come off his head and dangled down into the darkness. The radio had miraculously managed to stay clipped to his belt.

They had brought a rope, but it was in the pack by the desk in the basement, so he couldn't afford to drop into the darkness. Besides, Sugar wasn't here to haul him out.

His arm muscles bulged as he hoisted his body from the pit, glad for all those pushup pyramids he'd done for so long. Even still, he almost didn't make it. Rolling onto his side, he caught his breath while in the distance he could hear Russ saying, "Jackson? Jackson!" his voice tinny and muffled through the headset.

Jackson dragged the headset up by the cord and put it back on his head. "Never mind," he said, staggering to his feet before breaking into a cautious jog through the rest of the building to get the cart. "You need to tell me where she is."

"Looks like she's coming this direction," Russ said.

"Can you reach her?"

"Just static."

Without Russ guiding him, Jackson figured he could run in circles all night in the tunnels and never find her. "I'm coming to you. Keep following her and tell me which is the closest shop with tunnel access so I can get down there to find her."

"Roger," Russ said, his tone full of worry.

⟵

Sugar woke up, disoriented and groggy. For a few moments, she watched the dim overhead lighting as it passed, wondering what was going on. Then she remembered. Barbara tied to the wheelchair looking behind Sugar and everything going black.

There was a muffled squeal as wheels that needed to be oiled turned below her and she realized she was in a wheelchair as well, someone using it to move her through the tunnels. She sat uncomfortably slumped, rope tying her to the chair.

Straightening her head, she shut her eyes against the nausea and dizziness, then cracked her right eye open to see an empty hall. Someone, she assumed Niles, hauled her along backwards.

She took stock of her body, flexing feet and arms, fingers and toes. Each leg raised when she asked it to.

Everything worked and she found only her upper body was tied to the chair. Her radio headset was gone, as was the radio, but it would have been too much to ask that Niles had left it on her. The camera, however, was still clipped onto her shoulder.

Sugar had once read that if someone attacked you, your only chance of escape was before they had you isolated and at their mercy. She figured this was her only shot to break free before she was put someplace she'd be trapped.

She debated her options. There weren't a lot of things she could do tied to the wheelchair, but she figured Jackson would realize she was gone soon, which meant buying time was her best bet. Her lower body would have to be the catalyst, since her top was stuck.

Dropping her shoes onto the floor of the tunnel, she dragged her feet. The wheelchair came to an abrupt stop.

"What's happened here?" asked Niles in his rusty voice. "Feet must have fallen off."

Sugar closed her eyes, wanting him to get close so she could do some sort of kung fu move like in the movies.

Niles dragged one of her legs off the ground and put it back on the footrest.

Sugar tensed, ready to kick Niles in his old guy stomach.

"Mhhhh," said Barbara.

"What's wrong now?" Niles said, stepping away before Sugar could do any kung fu. "This is why I had to put a gag on you, Barbara. No one likes someone who won't shut up."

He must have pulled off the gag anyway, because a woman's voice said behind her, "Niles, you can't do this. People love Atlantis."

"Well *people* are wrong. *People* are what's wrong with the world, always polluting and ruining habitat."

"This isn't the way to fix things," Barbara said.

Sugar wondered how Niles was planning to fix things. That sounded ominous.

"The only way fish like Harold can survive is by getting rid of this abomination once and for all. I realize that now."

"You can't kill us," Barbara pleaded.

"I'm not going to kill you," Niles said, sounding insulted. "Even if the world would be better off, I'm a pacifist."

"Then where are you taking us?"

"To the submarine ride. I've set it free from its track and programmed it to go to the dock on shore before Atlantis explodes. This place has killed its last fish."

What the hell. She'd known from the beginning that Niles was nuts.

"Are you going to get all the Bachelor people in the sub?" Barbara asked.

"Yeah, although they keep escaping from my traps. I have three of them already, plus this one. That only leaves four to capture, although the big man is going to be hard to subdue. I will most likely need to use drastic measures, since the explosives are set."

Explosives! Holy crap. Sugar hoped like hell Russ could still see out of her camera somehow and was listening to this. He had to be, right? She had no idea, but the number one thing she had to do was free herself and warn the others.

Niles had made a mistake. He'd tied her onto the chair to keep her from falling off, not to keep her tied there. He must have thought she'd stay passed out until he got her on the submarine. While Niles and Barbara argued, she slowly worked the rope which tied her onto the chair up her arms.

"If you blow up Atlantis, you'll end up killing fish," Barbara pointed out.

"It has to be done. Once Atlantis is in tatters, the fish will use the wreckage to thrive and return to their old levels. That's what happened at Chernobyl."

"What does Chernobyl have to do with it?" Barbara asked, as confused as Sugar was.

Almost there. The rope wiggled over her shoulders, scraping her skin in the process.

"When all the people left Chernobyl, the wildlife came back. Species that were supposed to be extinct revived. They can thrive even with radiation, but not where people dwell." Niles had switched to a lecturing tone. "Do you understand how destructive people are?"

Sugar stood as silently as she could, but was still so woozy on her feet, that the wheelchair skidded out behind her and she ended up in a heap on the tunnel floor. "Shit," she said, rolling to try to stand again.

"No," Niles said, lunging for her.

She ducked, but her pocket caught on the wheelchair as she tried to gain her feet, the fabric ripping and her flashlight rolling free.

Niles' huge hands grabbed her, his face crazed.

CHAPTER SIXTEEN

Sugar fisted her hand and hit Niles in the stomach as hard as she could, yelling "Bam!" at the top of her lungs for some unknown reason.

The old man doubled over, letting out a whoosh.

From nowhere, Barbara smashed him over the head with the flashlight, the weight making a dull thud.

"Oh my God," Sugar said, looking at the old man on the floor, feeling horrible. "He's not dead is he?"

They both stared, the darkness making it hard to tell. They leaned forward to try to see.

"Ohhh," Niles moaned.

They both jumped backwards.

"Okay, good. We didn't kill him." She would have felt terrible if they had, although Niles *was* kidnapping her.

"What now?" Barbara asked.

Sugar pushed away the anxiety that wanted to overwhelm her. "We can't leave him." Even if it was tempting. "Let's put him in the wheelchair and find a way to the surface. I'm done being in these tunnels." Thank God Russ had put a tracker on her. Surely by now he and Jackson were coming to her rescue.

She dragged the wheelchair close. "On three," Sugar said, taking one arm with Barbara taking the other, making a still-woozy Niles moan. "One, Two, Three."

They heaved, but he immediately flunked back down

on the ground.

"He's a lot heavier than he looks," Sugar said, gasping for breath at the small exertion.

"My back," Barbara moaned.

"We can't leave him," Sugar said, secretly wishing they could.

"No, you're right," Barbara agreed, sounding disappointed but resigned.

It took a couple tries but they finally had him situated in the chair. Then they tied him with every bit of rope they had, since they didn't want him rising up and conking one of them on the head in retaliation. Not that he looked like he was in any shape to stand. Even when they dropped him, Niles only moaned.

"Which way is the fastest way out?"

"Follow me," Barbara said and limped back the way they'd come letting Sugar push the wheelchair. She stopped eventually in front of a door, taking out a key and opening it.

It took both of them to drag the wheelchair up the stairs, Sugar pulling backwards and Barbara pushing from below. When they made it through Bob's Billiards and onto the street, they were both heaving for breath.

"I should get a gym membership," Sugar said, grasping her knees and gasping for breath. But when was she ever home enough to use it? Really, she should take up running. She could run anywhere, no matter where they were filming. Too bad she hated being sweaty and in pain.

Down the road, an engine roared as Jackson came into view.

She straightened as he came to a halt. "Sure, now you show up," she said, but she was grinning at him. She wondered if the pleasure at the sight of him would ever fade.

He dismounted and in two giant strides picked Sugar up and spun her around. "I was so worried," he murmured into her neck before putting her down and stepping back.

His reaction made Sugar's heart clench. "I'm hard to

subdue."

"I was counting on it."

What if she got another job and left this life for him? He might be worth the sacrifice. He might be worth just about anything.

"If Niles has really rigged this place to blow up, we need to round up your crew and get into the submarine ride," Barbara said, bringing them back to the real world.

A world where Sugar had no marketable skills and was too old to start over. Besides, she loved her job. She was good at it. And her job had never left her for another woman or abandoned her when she was at a low point.

"We heard Niles threats. Think he's going to really do it?" Jackson asked Barbara.

"He's clearly gone insane. Or maybe he was always crazy. It's hard to tell." Barbara stared at Niles still strapped to his wheelchair. The old man gasped for breath even thought he hadn't been the one who'd had to haul the wheelchair up the steps.

Sugar had so many questions for him, but there would be plenty of time to ask them after they had everyone safe. "He said it will go off in two hours, but when the timer started is the question. We can't risk cutting it close."

"Russ can you grab the two remaining contestants and meet us at the submarine ride?" Jackson asked into his headset. "We're missing Cindy and the other two."

"Niles said he had three people there. Let's get Niles and Barbara to the sub and we can confirm the three of them are already on the ship," Sugar said, snapping into Head Wrangler mode. Prioritize and make it happen was the name of the game. This is what she excelled at—getting things done in the midst of adversity.

The two missing contestants were tied to wheelchairs, sitting on the platform waiting to be loaded, with a third man who turned out to be John.

Jillian had fallen over in her wheelchair and

floundered as they walked up. "About time you guys arrived," she snapped.

"We came as quickly as possible." Sugar said, working on Jillian's ropes which had tightened with all her struggles, while Jackson untied Andi and John in a flash.

Jackson righted Jillian's wheelchair so they could both work on the knots.

"Oh, you're so strong," she cooed.

"I quit the show," he said, the last knot giving way. "I'm no longer this season's Bachelor."

Jillian stood and dusted off her hands. "Then whatever with you." She turned to Sugar. "Who's the new bachelor?"

Sugar had no idea. "Atlantis is having system problems so we're going to take this submarine to the surface. Once we're there, Hank Carson will brief you." Sugar had no idea what Hank was going to do and at this point, she didn't care. They would all have to escape, then they could worry about the show.

It suddenly hit her that not even Hank Carson could save things this time. If the show failed, she might be finished as a wrangler. No one survived from this level of catastrophe without being tainted. It didn't matter that it wasn't her fault. It was her job to make things right and there was no making this right. The bachelor had quit. The four women who were stuck down here had gone off script.

Barbara, still shaky on her feet, was doing something over at the control panel that the ride operator would usually man.

That's when Sugar realized that Cindy was missing.

She spun around, then checked in the submarine, which turned out to be tiny. Five rows of two seats marched down the middle, with an operator/tour guide space up front. The ship was empty.

"Cindy," she said.

"Maybe she's with Russ?" Jackson stared down the

street where a golf cart could be seen rounding the corner.

Sugar's stomach tightened as she counted only three people, one in the driver's seat and two crammed next to him.

Sugar took off to meet them, Jackson at her heels. "Have you seen Cindy?"

Russ shook his head. "I thought she'd be with you?"

"Have everyone board the sub and prepare to leave. We'll go back and check the apartments," Sugar said, but she had a bad feeling since she'd already looked there for Cindy before all of this had started. "A woman who can't walk couldn't have gotten far."

"Let's ask Niles first. If he truly is a pacifist, then he won't want her to die." Jackson strode up to Niles and knelt down before him, speaking quietly, probably so the other contestants wouldn't be worried.

"She's in the Physical Plant, on the first floor." Niles' voice rang out making everyone else fall silent. "You have to get her. My timer says we only have twenty-five minutes until the charges go off and we have to be far away or the explosion will rip the submarine apart."

"I'll get her," Jackson said, but Sugar beat him to the golf cart.

"I'll drive." This was her job and she wasn't going to leave anyone behind.

They peeled off, tires spinning and laying rubber.

"Left, left," Jackson said, grabbing the edge of the roof as she took the turn way too fast.

The Physical Plant loomed ahead of them, but when they raced to the front door, it was locked again.

⌣

Jackson felt like he'd missed his calling. A life of crime would have given him the adventure he craved and he'd have actually made money at it. Instead, he was currently broke, unemployed, and in love with a woman who didn't want him.

He pushed the negative thoughts out of his mind to concentrate.

His hands were rock solid without a single tremor as he picked the lock, then they were inside, Sugar calling for Cindy.

No answer.

"If she was able to call to us, we would have heard her when we were here earlier." Jackson stared at the map on the wall. "We know she isn't on the way to the basement stairs we used. We'll need to split up and check either side."

Sugar nodded, spinning on one foot and racing to the western part of the building, while Jackson took the east. It didn't take long until he'd tried every room in his half.

He retraced his steps to the other side of the building. "Sugar?" he called, a bad feeling gathering in his gut. She should have been finishing her search about the time he did. The building wasn't that large.

"Jackson!"

Her muffled voice came from somewhere to the left, the tone so filled with panic, he stumbled forward, almost falling headlong into yet another trap.

Pinwheeling his arms, he managed to toss himself backward rather than fall into the hole.

"There's a hole," Sugar said unhelpfully from below.

He sat down hard on his ass. "Yeah I see that." Across the room Cindy moaned, still in the wheelchair he'd rigged up for her, eyes huge with a piece of silver tape across her mouth and a large piece taping her to the chair.

"Should I try to find a way out?" Sugar asked from the hole. "There is access to the tunnel."

"We don't have time for you to get lost." Then he remembered their pack down in the basement. "Let me grab the rope." He stood and hustled to the basement steps.

"What rope?" she called after him.

He didn't bother to remind her. Time was ticking down.

The pack still sat beside the desk, the manual still open to the page he'd been reading when he realized Sugar was missing. The rope still sat helpfully on top. He grabbed it and was back up in a flash. Tying a knot in the end for her to stand on, he lowered the rope. "Hold on," he said, then put his back into it, wishing he had more leverage. Hand over hand, he hauled her up until she could grasp the floorboards, then he knelt down and ungracefully wrestled her out. They had no time to catch their breath. Instead, he circled the edge of the room and rolled Cindy carefully around the edge.

"Niles has set explosives to go off in twenty minutes. We have to go as fast as possible," Sugar told her.

Jackson ripped the tape from around Cindy as fast as he could, freeing her from the wheelchair. Sugar helped him lift her into the cart, time ticking away. He drove like a bat out of hell down the road, wondering if the others had left them. If they had, there wasn't time for another plan. They would die here. He'd always thought he'd die in a space accident, not at an amusement park.

"Come on!" Russ cried from the platform, racing down to carry Cindy up for him, while Jackson grabbed Sugar's hand and hauled her into the submarine.

"Hurry before we die," Jillian shouted unhelpfully from the back, as Russ safely stowed Cindy in a seat.

Jackson and Sugar dropped into the front row, their breath chugging in and out of their lungs at their close escape.

A bell rang as the door slowly, oh so slowly shut.

"Everyone buckle up," Sugar shouted and Jackson could hear metal clangs as the contestants followed her directions.

"Faster!" someone screamed, saying what they all were thinking.

"This isn't supposed to be a real submarine. It's a ride to see fish," Barbara protested, but the sub growled as she guided it away from the dock and pushed it to its max.

"Fifteen minutes," Niles said, his rusty voice full of

panic. "We're too close. We're going to die."

"Position the sub so it's going straight up," Jackson said, and hit a lever that jerked everyone back in their seats.

They crawled up towards the surface.

"Can't we go faster?" Jillian yelled.

"This sub is made to keep us from getting the bends. It won't go any faster."

They continued to crawl to the surface.

The explosion ripped through the water behind them, a wave slapping into them, sending them shooting upwards, so fast their ears popped and they all screamed. Too quickly, they surfaced, the engines grinding on air when they were intended to work in water.

The sub slapped down into the water, dipping below the surface before bobbing back up again.

Heavy breathing filled the cabin as everyone tried to catch their breath. Jackson realized the silence meant that the engines had shut down. He gently moved Barbara from her seat and tried to restart them. They chugged and coughed, but didn't catch. Someone would have to rescue them but at least they were safe on the surface.

Forget space, Jackson thought, *if I want adventure, I should join the crew on a reality TV show.*

He and Barbara radioed for help, then sat down to wait, giving him a chance to ask a question that had been puzzling him the whole time he'd been in Atlantis. "One thing I have to know. Why all the trapdoors?"

"None of us knew. Some of the staff figured the original owner was completely crazy," Barbara said weakly. "All of the doors had been padlocked for safety."

"Niles must have taken them off." Sugar turned to stare at the old man, who ignored her to gaze out the window at the view, probably thinking about fish.

It took hours, but finally the coast guard towed them into the dock. Enough time for Jackson to contemplate the fact he only had one life to live and he better live it to the fullest. This close call had been a warning.

He stood on the dock, breathing in and out, enjoying the rising sun as it came over the horizon. It had been one hell of a night.

Sugar came to stand beside him. "We almost died," she said, her voice subdued. She held her cellphone in her hands limply.

"We did." He turned to meet her gaze. He wanted to ask her to choose him. He wanted to insist that he was the right man for her and he was worth more than her job, but he didn't.

Sugar wasn't even looking at him. Instead, she watched Hank Carson hurrying down the dock towards them. "I don't think any employer would hold this against me," she said softly.

She was still thinking about her job, still hoping to salvage her career.

Well, he wasn't going to stand between her and what she wanted. Besides, he deserved a woman who would sacrifice for him the way he was willing to sacrifice for her. "When you finally realize how special this thing is between us, you should call me," he said, taking her phone and inputting his number into her contacts. "I'm worth it."

For a moment, she looked away from Hank. "Jackson," she said, but didn't say anything more.

Well, that was an answer in itself, wasn't it? "I'll see you later, Sugar," he said, shaking his head when she didn't even seem to hear him.

"Sugar." Hank wove his way around Jillian who had planted herself in front of him, probably to interrogate him on who the next bachelor would be. "Atlantis." He stared out into the water.

"Is gone." Sugar's voice was still vague and distant.

Hank turned to Jackson and straightened, already reaching acceptance on the loss and pivoting to the next issue. "Have you really quit?"

"I really have."

"He saved all our lives. You should hire him as a Fixer," Sugar said, trying to smooth things over.

Jackson didn't even bother to ask what a Fixer was. He wanted to leave, go someplace and hole up and lick his wounded heart.

Hank gave him a close look as if he actually considered it. "A Fixer makes a fraction of what the Bachelor was offered."

"It turns out no money in the world is worth being the Bachelor," Jackson said. He clapped Carson on the back. "I'll see you later, Sugar," he said, but he was beginning to suspect he wouldn't.

He walked up the dock and out of her life. He hoped not forever.

CHAPTER SEVENTEEN

Sugar stood in front of a 1920's Victorian, surprised that this was where Jackson Wright chose to live. It looked like the old house was held together by staples and duct tape, if the beat-up front wrap-around porch was any indication.

Behind the scenes, she'd orchestrated Jackson's hiring as the Fixer for the filming of the first season of Hank Carson's new reality TV show *Treasure: Hitler's Hidden Tunnels*. This show, about teams of two who compete to find legendary treasure, was a huge departure from Hank's usual Love TV, but Hank, being Hank, had talked the producers into bankrolling it, adding another feather to his cap.

Since Hank was now producing a second show every year, he needed a second Head Wrangler. He'd hired Sugar for two reasons. First, she had the chops, but he'd also he felt bad about the screw job he'd done to her career by leaving her in Atlantis for days unsupported in a no-win situation. He hadn't even yelled at her for kissing Jackson, maybe because the footage had been thrown out before it was discovered. Or maybe by the time Hank saw it, he'd switched his focus to his brilliant solution, pulling off another win, this time one that probably would get him the accolades he'd always been after. He'd turned Atlantis into a documentary that the whole world had tuned in to see, including interviews with the cast and even a long, passionate interview with Niles about the state of fishing preservation in the United States. Ecoterrorism, it turned out, was riveting to the American public.

The first thing Sugar had suggested for the new show was that Hank hire Jackson as the show's Fixer. She needed to figure out exactly how they were going to function on set. She was sure he'd moved on after that day on the dock, but she hadn't. She'd spent the last month holed up in her apartment, staring at his number, trying to figure out what to do. She'd almost called him twice to apologize, but what was she apologizing for? Not picking him over her career? Did she owe him an apology for that? She didn't think so. She'd been in shock on the dock when he'd strode away, not giving her a chance to think about what to say or do. Once the close call was over, she'd gone off the rails in relief, but only for a short time. She'd regained her sanity but by then, he was gone. If she'd had her wits about her, she would have said... she wasn't sure.

That she wanted him. That she needed him to be happy.

But it had all happened too fast and he'd left without giving her time to speak.

Then Hank had taken over and they'd raced around trying to get the documentary made and do all the extra interviews. Hank had done the ones with Jackson, so she hadn't even seen him like she'd expected. Hank had to provide a certain number of episodes to fulfill the contract and they'd really had to stretch to make the new show *Terror in Atlantis* work. They'd somehow pulled it off and they'd had a decent amount of people watching, although certainly not the same amount as they would have had with The Bachelor.

When Jackson had accepted the job as the Fixer for the new show, she decided she couldn't work with him without knowing how he felt. Avoiding things between them was no longer an option. She'd stolen his address from his new hire paperwork and here she was.

She took a breath and walked up the rickety stairs. Somewhere deep inside the house, a hammer banged away, hard at work.

Last chance to lame out. She pressed the bell before she could change her mind.

Nothing happened.

She pressed it again, harder this time, but still, nothing.

She banged on the door at increasing volume until the hammer stopped. The old beautiful stained glass in the center of the door showed the outline of a huge body moving down the hall.

Jackson opened the door, his eyes widening a little but otherwise his face was blank. "Took your time contacting me," he said, leaning against the doorframe. He'd cut his hair even shorter than it had been on set, but his body was even more muscled out.

A small shiver of need went through her. *Mine*, her body said, but she beat off the need to fling herself at him, even as a visceral memory of running her hands down his perfect chest filled her with the desire to fling off her clothing and launch herself at him.

"Yeah," she answered, knowing that wasn't very intelligent sounding, but out of the many things she'd expected him to say when he spoke to her again, that wasn't it. She'd anticipated more of a reaction. Anger or irritation or maybe even happiness. Plus, the need to touch him again was filling her head up, dropping her IQ and stealing her words.

"We're working together," he said. "I'm assuming I have you to thank for the job offer."

She shrugged a shoulder. "Running around in tunnels looking for treasure while dealing with old Nazi booby-traps seemed right up your alley."

"It did appeal to me. You're the Head Wrangler?"

"I am."

A slow pirate smile spread across his lips. "Guess you can't duck out of dealing with what's between us any longer."

Her stomach tumbled with a combination of need and happiness at being in his presence. His cool reception kept her from gushing out an apology. She didn't want to mess this up again. This might be her last chance to get this right. "I guess I can't."

He raised an eyebrow. "Want to have sex before or after we talk about how we're going to manage this on set?" he asked, gesturing between the two of them.

Her lips parted into an "Oh," as she struggled to process the sudden change in direction, but her insides jumped straight into the pit of desire that had been growing at the mere sight of him. "Before?" she asked, wishing the word wasn't quite so breathy. This wasn't wise, but she'd been wise her whole life, so fuck it.

"You're wish is my command," he said, and before she realized what he was going to do, he swept her into his arms, caught the door with his heel and slammed it closed.

"Nice house," she commented as he took the stairs two at a time.

"Thanks, it's my current project to keep my busy until you decided to show back up in my life."

Her heart turned over. "You were waiting for me?" The hope in the words embarrassed her, but she wanted him.

"Sugar, I would wait for you forever if you made me. Luckily, I didn't have to wait that long."

Wow, he wasn't beating around the bush about his feelings.

They entered a beautiful, refinished room, the ceilings stretching up ten feet, big windows marching across the far wall, a massive king-sized bed taking up the majority of the space. "This is gorgeous," she said, staring at the tin ceiling and ornate chair rail.

"I took the trunk room next door and turned it into a bath-room and closet for you."

He'd built this room for her. She wanted to run her hands along the carved, polished oak of the massive mantel over the fireplace, explore the bathroom he'd built for her, but there were more important things to do first. "You must have been sure I was coming."

He tossed her onto the bed making her yip, then followed her down. "Why wouldn't you? We're perfect for each other." Then his lips were on hers.

Sugar's stomach turned over with need and joy. This man was a homecoming. This was what she wanted, more than a career and more than anything else in her life. She kissed him with her heart and soul, rolling him to his back so she could straddle him.

He tugged off her shirt as she struggled to pull his up over his shoulders. He sat so she could take off his shirt. She tossed it behind her to feast her eyes on the muscles of his chest. Somehow they'd become harder and more defined, although if you'd asked her before, she would have thought that was an impossible feat.

Sunlight streamed into the room, giving her the lighting she hadn't had the last time they'd been together. She ran her hands along his chest, enjoying how his muscles tightened under her touch. Her mouth followed, and she kissed along his skin, as he unhooked her bra with one flick of the wrist. She shimmied free and dipped her chest to graze the tips of her bare nipples across the expanse of his gorgeous chest.

He brought her breasts up to eye level. "I've been dreaming of this moment where I see you naked. I missed out on last time." Then his mouth was on her right nipple, sucking the way she'd remembered from before, when she'd spent lonely nights thinking of him touching her.

This, *this* was what she wanted, needed, had to have. God, she'd had him once and she never wanted anyone else again.

He took his time, suckling one breast, then the other until she moaned from the need building inside her. Part of her wondered if she would come just from his mouth on her breasts alone, especially when his hand trailed along the tops of her jeans, teasingly dipping below the edge.

Suddenly, he sat up and leaned over to open a drawer beside the bed, catching her easily as she started to topple. "Unless you're against it, I think we'll need these," he said, handing her the pack of condoms.

The pause was enough for her to regain her thinking brain. She wanted this to last forever. She wasn't going to let him race her to the finish. "Not yet. I've been thinking about your body for a month now. I want to touch every inch of your hot man flesh."

He laughed and laid back. "It's all yours."

"Then I need to see it all." She tugged off his pants to his ankles, dropped to kneel on the floor to tug off his work boots.

"You are so beautiful," he said, staring down at her.

She let her gaze roam the line of his now naked body. "You are too."

He tipped a slow grin at her. "Men aren't beautiful."

"You are." She started to climb on him, but he shook his head.

"Your pants. It's only fair, plus I want your wonderful nakedness all over me."

Feeling a momentary flash of self-consciousness, she pulled off her jeans and climbed back on the bed. Then the feelings faded as she ran her hands from his shoulders to his feet. He really was perfect. No wonder Hank had thought he'd make such a great bachelor.

They kissed, exploring each other's mouths, tongues tangling, discovering each other like they hadn't been able to before, when touching was off limits and they'd been fighting against their basic natures. She'd never realized how much she liked to kiss, how much she craved it. He was excellent at it, too. His mouth firm yet soft, teasing her into wanting more.

She took her time licking along his body, skirting around his rather amazing-looking cock to taste her way along the curve of his hip.

"Sugar," he gasped, and she relished it. This was what she'd wanted all along. This man lying under her, moaning her name.

His hands kept up a steady exploration, dipping in between the folds of her sex to tease the tight bud at the apex of her thighs, pushing her firmly out of patience.

She needed him to fill her up, as deeply as possible.

Scrambling through the now wrinkled bedspread below them, she found the condoms and rolled one in place.

"Thank God," he moaned. "I couldn't take much more of that."

She straddled him and fitted the tip of his cock into her passage. Working slowly, she inched up and down, slowly seating him inside her while he moaned beneath her. "You're killing me, woman," he said.

"You don't look dead yet," she murmured, the power of being totally in control of this amazing man below her making her even more turned on. This was it. This was everything she'd ever wanted.

⌒

Jackson stared at the women on top of him, his cock deep inside her. He'd never wanted anyone like he did Sugar. She meant more to him than anything, including space.

He'd almost given up hope that she would come to him. Jackson had known he had to wait for her, but his patience was gravely wearing thin and he'd begun to plot ways that he could accidentally bump into her. She'd obviously avoided him at the last round of filming, never joining any of the interviews or calling to talk about the show. If she wasn't going to come to him, maybe he'd have to remind her just what she was missing.

It wasn't until Hank Carson offered him the job as the Fixer for his new series that a spark of renewed hope had blossomed. He'd asked who the Head Wrangler was and when Hank said it was Sugar, Jackson wondered if she'd finally come to the conclusion he'd know from the minute he'd ridden down the elevator with her that first day. They were meant to be together.

During that very long two weeks, he'd worked on this bedroom, picturing Sugar here with every modification. He wanted her in every way, not just for quick sex. He wanted to wake up in the morning beside her, go to bed every night curled into her arms—for the rest of his life.

She started slow, not raising her hips but more moving across him.

He tried to distract himself so he wouldn't come too soon. He needed this to be perfect and not ruin it by leaving her behind. He didn't want her to second guess the fact they were destined to be together. She was his soulmate. He would do anything to please her.

He held onto her hips just to keep a grip on reality as she set a gruelingly slow pace. An ache deep inside him began to grow, building more and more like water on a dam, until a tremor shook through him.

Then her body picked up speed and the pleasure rushed from his head to his toes, so right, he wanted to scream to let out some of the building tension.

Finally, finally, Sugar moaned, "Oh God," writhing above him mindlessly as she climaxed.

The tight leash he kept on his body was freed and he flipped their positions so she was below him, moving his cock in and out, once, twice, then he was coming while she continued to shiver around him.

They collapsed together, both breathing like they'd run a marathon.

He rolled free and gathered her close, his body sated but his mind still unsure. "Are you sure you want to work together?"

Her head flopped over toward him as if she was barely able to control her body. "Neither of us report to the other. You're in charge of your staff, I'm in charge of mine. We have to coordinate, but we shouldn't be in conflict very often."

He trailed one finger along her perfect jawline. "I don't want this job as much as I want you."

She grinned. "We don't have to choose, Jackson. We can have our jobs and each other. I'm sure of it." She captured his hand and held it tight. "Unless you only want to live in space? I am not saying never, but for now, I need to stay on Earth and I want you to be with me."

"I'm okay with staying for now, as long as you consider it in the future if the possibility presents itself." There was a piece of him that still wanted space so badly, but he knew and accepted that now wasn't the time. He wanted Sugar. He was willing to wait—hell, he was willing to never go to space if it meant he could have her.

"I promise if you get an opportunity, I'll work hard to make it happen. I know you want it."

"I do," he said. "But not more than I want you." He pressed a kiss onto her hand. "I love you, you know."

"I love you too. I tried to fight it, but it's a fact I'll have to live with."

He kissed her deep, feeling need stirring again inside him. He thrilled at the thought that they had the rest of their lives to have sex together.

The whole path of his life shifted before him, filled with lost treasures, adventure, and best of all Sugar.

THE END

About the Author

Leigh Wyndfield lives in rural Virginia with her fat cat Ayra, two lovable rescue puppies, four chickens, and the best guy in the world. A city girl at heart, she's embracing the mysteries of growing things and watching deer race from hunters through her yard. Traveling and driving an ambulance round out her time. She writes romance fiction that is out of this world.

To learn more about Leigh Wyndfield, please visit https://leighwyndfield.com/contact.html#newsletter and join her newsletter list!

www.ingramcontent.com/pod-product-compliance
Lightning Source LLC
Chambersburg PA
CBHW050446110726
47899CB00003B/833